Products of the Streets

A Novel by
Demonde "Money" Anderson

First Edition August 2023

Printed in the United States of America

Lock Down Publications
P.O. Box 944
Stockbridge, GA 30281
www.lockdownpublications.com

Like our page on Facebook: Lock Down Publications
www.facebook.com/lockdownpublications.ldp

Stay Connected with Us!

Text LOCKDOWN to 22828 to stay up-to-date with new
releases, sneak peaks, contests and more…
Or CLICK HERE to sign up.

Like our page on Facebook:
Lock Down Publications: Facebook

Join Lock Down Publications/The New Era Reading Group

Visit our website:
www.lockdownpublications.com

Follow us on Instagram:
Lock Down Publications: Instagram

Email Us: We want to hear from you!

Dedication

All praise and Glory is to Allah, Master of the Worlds, and Ruler of the Day of Judgement. I would like to dedicate this book to everyone who stuck through with me no matter the hardships we may have along the way. Y'all know what it is, for every hundred y'all gave it'll always be the same in return ... 100/100!

Acknowledgements

I want to thank every single individual who had a hand in making this dream of mine come true. I always had a passion for writing and y'all always had a passion for rocking with me and for that I appreciate y'all. And for everyone that had a hand in bringing this book to life, I thank you too, but we're just getting started ... LOL!

Prologue

"Max, bring me the envelope from the car," Mr. Mackmillions spoke with a deep southern baritone.

Mr. Mackmillions was doing what he did best, earning his status while adding to the extraordinary legend behind his name, which would live on in the hood like that of a great musical icon or that of a Hall of Fame sports star. Business was his forte, and he loved everything about it: the money, the knowledge, and the reflection of the amazing standings in which standard he was able to live and provide for his organization and family, being in the ranks of the upper echelon of his era.

The lavish and luxurious style he adorned in the way he dressed and carried himself, coupled with the selfless way he loved and cared to give back to his community, was like nothing the streets of Houston had ever seen before him. His elegance and grace defined the handsome and generous man. Mackentosh Miller knew the ins and outs of the city and beyond, and he would do anything to keep it that way.

"Well, Mr. Miller, I hope everything is as you pleased with this fine property," Marcus Blackwell, owner and CEO of BW Realtors, stated while joyously looking over the contract they'd just signed.

"Of course it is, Marcus, why else do you think my signature is on those documents?" Mr. Mackmillions replied while signaling to Max.

Max was a professional killer who loved the art of his own kills. His skills and loyalty were given to only one person, and Mr. Mackmillions always showed his appreciation.

Marcus Blackwell had played the game well, almost without a flaw, but he'd played his hand too close to his chest by conning two of Mr. Mackmillions' most profitable clients, and signing his name on the line of that contract was in fact him signing away his own life.

Max moved as swift as the wind, covering the three feet of space between him and his victim, and Blackwell wouldn't have seen it coming if he'd been staring in a mirror. The razor thin wire in Max's grip constricted around Blackwell's throat, drawing blood instantly. His fingers desperately clawed his neck in search of the wire deeply penetrating his flesh with every painful jerk and twist of his body. He didn't want to move but the lack of oxygen to his lungs and brain involuntarily caused his limbs to shake.

"Pl—Pleassseee—" His voice sounded in a gargled whisper.

"Please what?" Mr. Mackmillions stepped closer to the dying realtor.

"Pleasss—"

Mr. Mackmillions tapped twice on Max's shoulder, ordering him to release Blackwell from his death clutch.

"Now you want to be civil?" Mackmillions chuckled as he looked down on the pathetic man.

He hated how people had the nuts to use you up then cry about it when it was time to face the music. He respected men with dignity, strong balls, with a sense of acceptance and understanding to the fact that their actions came with severe consequences.

"You peeled tens of millions of U.S. dollars from my clients who thought it better to settle this issue with your death. I cannot say that I blame them one bit, but your simple death will only satisfy their thirst for revenge. Now you've willingly and knowingly, might I add, despite vividly knowing my reputation, tried to play me like one would a cheap rookie whore working a strip." Mr. Mackmillions gritted his teeth in anger before slapping spittle mixed with blood from Blackwell's mouth.

"I—I can—explain, let me explain," Blackwell struggled to get his words past his lips while Max tightened his death grip on the wire around his neck.

"Explanations are for people who care to know why something has taken place, but me Marcus, I don't-give-a-shit!" Mr. Mackmillions said between landing blow after blow to Blackwell's face and neck with the butt of his gold plated .44 automatic.

"See, Max, that's how you do shit, observe that shit right there then take pictures for the guys," Mr. Mackmillions ordered.

The brutal attack he delivered came at the request of some big guns in the upper echelons of power, influential men who believed in balance and stability; men who understood the nature of violence distributed by their contemporaries in the underworld.

"Cut his head off in live footage; that's where our big pay comes in with the hefty tips you like." Max loved the sound of more cash flowing through his hands to do things that—before meeting Mr. Mackmillions—he'd done for free or just to eat. With him it wasn't about the money at all; it was absolutely about the thrill from the kill that kept him excited.

Mackentosh "Mr. Mackmillions" Miller was a man cut from a special cloth, cloth as rare as America's black presidency. Many respected him, others never lived long after disrespecting him, but he was one humble being, always humble and never not humble even in times of tribulation.

"Take your time with wetting this place, we need it to burn to the ashes," Mr. Mackmillions ordered before leaving out to wait for Max in the car.

After spending time discussing contract agreements and matters of securities with his political connections, Mr.

Mackmillions stepped into his mansion in deep transformation. At home he was no longer Mr. Mackmillions, he was simply, Mackentosh Miller Sr., father and husband, his most favorite positions in life.

"Welcome home, my king," he heard Sylvia—his wife's voice—as he made it up the stairs where she stood waiting.

"Good to be back," he said, kissing her lips.

"Finally," she chuckled as their foreheads connected the way they always did when they missed each other.

"What are you doing up this time of night?" he asked, looking deep into her eyes.

"Waiting for you with our prince. He's been asking about his most favorite person in the whole world," Sylvia smiled before seductively kissing his lips again.

"Don't start nothing," he warned with a huge smile of his own.

"I'm definitely trying to, so after you give our prince his time, know what the queen needs hers too." Sylvia was a dime in every sense of the word, and Mackentosh loved and appreciated her more than anyone or anything in the world. She was his world along with their only child, Mackentosh Miller Jr.

"Don't go too far—I'd hate to have to find you in this big ass house you love so much," he playfully warned her.

"Scouts honor," Sylvia saluted, knowing he'd love nothing more than the opposite.

He leaned in and kissed her sexy full lips before giving her ass a nice swat as she sashayed off. He watched as she seductively teased him before disappearing at the end of the long hallway. The attraction between the two radiated effortlessly; they simply just enjoyed each other.

He removed his shoulder-holstered twin .44 automatics before stepping inside of his son's room. He calmed himself, therefore preparing his mind to expand that of his baby boy. He loved dropping jewels of important life knowledge on his son and later quizzing him about it.

"'Sup, dad!" Young Mack yelled in excitement before rushing his father.

"Whooa-haha!" Mackentosh laughed, enjoying his son's playful physicality. He was a strong eight-year-old, and Mackentosh planned to keep his mind just as strong as his body.

"Come on, you know what time it is, mind over matter."

"But I miss you and I wanna play with you, dad," Young Mack whined.

"Is that what I think it is?" Mackentosh asked his son.

"No, it's a real one this time," Young Mack tried his hand with his father.

"You don't think I know a fake tear when I see one, junior? I'm the one who taught you how to do that, now get over here," Mackentosh laughed while lifting Young Mack in the air and spinning him around over his head.

"Okay, okay, I'm ready." Young Mack laughed as his father sat him down on the foot of his bed before sitting next to him.

"I need to grow my money right, so I come to your office and drop one million dollars' cash on your desk and ask you to grow it under fifteen percent interest for an entire year, what does a year yield for my money?"

"Come on, dad, you never gave me one so hard before," Young Mack complained. He hated to give his father the wrong answers.

"Get out your pen and paper and solve it before you go to sleep."

"One hundred and fifty thousand a year, I got you!" Young Mack laughed and tried to escape before his father grabbed him but failed.

Mackentosh laughed while attacking his son with a volley of tickles all over his midsection. Young Mack loved his father's attention, craved it even at times, and at his young age he very much understood how important it was to have his father in his life. A lot of his peers at school told their teachers about them missing their fathers, but Young Mack couldn't relate nor could he understand how a father would willingly leave his child to grow up and fend for himself in this world. He was truly grateful that he wasn't experiencing the life altering situations that so many of his peers were. His father was his everything, and he looked up to him in every way imaginable.

"Alright—alright, you win," Young Mack yelled in excitement, hoping his father would let up on his assault.

"Say uncle," Mackentosh playfully demanded.

"Never!"

"You better say it before you pee yourself."

"I am Mackentosh Miller the second and I will never yield!" Young Mack roared. His struggles paid off as he twisted and was able to turn, finally escaping his father's magical fingers.

"You know I love you more than anything, right?"

"Yes, sir, and I love you too, dad," Young Mack said with a chest full of air.

Mackentosh smiled at his boy; he was the spitting image of himself, and it amazed him how much they were alike at heart.

"No matter what you go through in life, son, I want you to think with this," Mackentosh said, touching his son's temple.

"And never confuse those thoughts with feelings from here," he added, touching his chest over his heart.

"You understand me?"

"Yes, sir," Young Mack replied, looking up at his father, role model and super hero.

"Okay, I'll hold you to it. Now have you taken care of your hygiene?"

"Of course, dad, see," Young Mack gave him a quick breath sample and a smell under his young arms.

"That's my boy. Come on, it's bedtime. You have school in the morning."

Mackentosh took his time tucking his son into bed, then sat a while until he fell asleep. He never would understand why his son loved a bed so big and why his wife loved a house so grand, but whatever their desires were, he'd break his back for them to have them.

After killing the lights and leaving the door ajar, he left his son's room and went searching for his other reason for living. He was sure she was feeling some type of way when he arrived, and she managed to rock his shit up. Now he was gonna make her pay for that in the most sensual and painful way.

"Sylvia, baby, where are you?" he said aloud as he checked room after room and door after door for her.

He looked everywhere for her before finally realizing that he already knew where she was hiding herself and waiting for him to find her. His excitement grew as he descended the stairs, by-passing the living room. He stepped past their huge kitchen before making it to the door of their basement. It was there that they decided to make their home gym, and Sylvia loved the bench press more than any other piece of equipment, more because of the positions it allowed him to work her insides while she lay there.

He smiled once he heard the sound of slow jams coming from the basement. He knew she'd be in there waiting. He twisted the knob, and the door opened but there were no lights on as he made his way down into the gym to get to his queen.

12

He froze suddenly halfway down the steps from the awkward, murky feeling that something wasn't right. His heart began to pound against his chest as he stood there thinking about the weapons he'd left outside his son's room door.

"Sylvia, baby, you good?" Mackentosh said before taking another step.

Lights immediately shined, blinding him from the brightness and causing him to stop in his tracks, confused to what was going on.

"Freeze!"

"Don't move, muthafucker!"

"FBI!"

Those were the last words he remembered hearing before his world turned black from the tremendous blow to the back of his head from one of the agent's service weapons

Fuck, he thought to himself as thoughts of his wife setting him up crowded his already darkened state of mind.

Chapter One

"Drive this muthafucka, Ash!" Young Mack yelled as the red and blue squad car lights lit up behind them.

"Hook a left here. Rob, can you get a good hit on 'em?"

"Only one way to find out, bruh!" Rob sneered, then let his mack spit.

Bok! Bok! Bok! Bok! Bok! Bok! Bok!

"How 'bout that!" Rob exclaimed.

Young Mack and Ashton smiled as they watched the HPD cruiser collide with a row of cars parked on the side of the street. They knew the call for backup was already in and they needed to get rid of the second squad car before more caught on to their trail.

Ashton swung a quick left, then another right, hoping to lose the squad car, but the officer behind the wheel was driving like he was experienced through the Indy 500.

"Take Ennis Street and get us to the Bricks, asap!" Young Mack instructed before hanging out of the front passenger side window of their stolen Nissan Pathfinder.

Thew! Thew! Thew! Thew! Thew! Thew! Thew! Thew!

"I hate you hoes!" Young Mack spit as he sat back.

Rob whistled as Young Mack's trigger play went on display. They watched the second squad car swerve recklessly after it's hood exploded into flames and slammed into its windshield. The person behind the wheel soon lost control and crashed into a book store off the side of the street.

"That's what the fuck I'm talking 'bout, right there!" Ash yelled while whipping the stolen vehicle like a pro.

"Take a right," Young Mack ordered as they approached the Bricks.

They kept a close eye on the streets as they neared their stash car. They knew the streets didn't much talk to police but with the way that things were moving on social media, Young Mack wasn't trying to take any chances. Ashton pulled into a narrow breeze-way and parked before Young Mack jumped out and quickly headed for the can of gasoline he'd stashed there, and got to work soaking the stolen vehicle. Rob took to the streets and kept watch over them while his crew did their business. Ashton grabbed their winnings and loaded them into the stash car's trunk just as Young Mack started the blaze and hopped into the passenger seat next to him with Rob taking up the back.

"Now drive this mufucka like you got some sense," Young Mack smiled at his crew and couldn't wait to count their winnings and report to his father that everything was everything.

***

"Fifty apiece!" Rob was livid. This was their biggest payout since he and Ashton joined with Young Mack, and their take still wasn't to his liking. Ashton didn't care either way because this job put more money into his pockets than he'd ever had at one time. He wasn't complaining, but he felt for Rob though he wasn't about to speak on it.

Young Mack stared at Rob and saw the disappointment that he too felt. Young Mack was angry and knew he'd have to take things up with his old man about the way things were turning out on the scores. They needed bigger bang for their buck.

"Calm down. I understand how you're feeling and I'll bring it up when I go see my pops." Young Mack tried covering his own disdain as he finished wrapping the stacks of money he'd be dropping off for his father.

"Yeah, right! You go telling yo ol' man how I feel and I'll be looking for work on another team as soon as those words leave your lips," Rob stated, knowing Mr. Mackmillions would feel slighted by his uneasiness with their payouts.

"If you've never said anything smart in your life, you just did then," Ashton laughed, dropping his cut into his Goyard gym bag next to him on the sofa. He sat back and fired up the kush weed and listened to the others.

Young Mack thought about what Rob had said and found his words to be pin-point accurate because his father hated a greedy man, but he had to do something. He knew Rob wasn't being greedy. Things were hot on their asses this go around, and two cops may be seriously injured or dead behind this take. Rob was right: fifty grand wasn't shit for the amount of work that came with this last job.

"Look, don't sweat this shit, I'll speak on our behalves when I go see pops." Young Mack decided, knowing he had to have his men's back on this issue.

"Thanks, you know you my dude, right?" Rob said, slapping fist with Young Mack and Ashton. "I think it's time for me to raise up outta here, got a few cuties that require some hair, nail, and body treatments." Rob laughed as he walked to the door stuffing his pockets with his portion of their winnings.

Boom!

"Get on the floor and put your hands behind your fucking heads!" someone yelled after dismantling the front door. Rob was too slow to get out of the way and found himself slammed between the door and the hard floor. Young Mack and Ashton scrambled but froze in their tracks from the sounds of bullets being chambered.

"Arghhh, man get off of me," Rob groaned very much in pain as each man stepped on the door to enter the cramped old house.

Rob remained pinned to the floor as he watched his friends do as they were ordered. At first sight, their attackers looked to be law enforcers, but the masked faces and zip ties being forced on his friends' wrists and ankles told him something different.

The boys in blue would be after our heads, Rob thought to himself as he looked on.

Young Mack was furious. He lay motionless watching everything unfold right before his eyes. The men dressed in HPD uniforms with detective badges hanging from their necks were ransacking their spot, looking for something. He wasn't fooled by their get ups though; he knew they were being robbed. Looking from Ashton over to Rob, he could see the same thing in both their eyes; they were on to the fake detectives as well. His blood churned because this was a very low-key location on a dead-end street that no one bothered to occupy, and by the looks of things these men knew exactly what they were looking for. The thought alone angered him more.

"I'm only gonna ask this once, fellas, and I expect you to tell me what I wanna hear. I shouldn't have to warn you what it will mean for the three of you if you don't." Young Mack kept his eyes on the masked man speaking. "Tell me where the money is."

Young Mack never took his eyes off the guy that was doing all the talking, because something was familiar about him. Something very familiar but Young Mack just couldn't place him. Deep down, Young Mack truly feared for his life and the lives of his men, but being in the game that they were in, he knew he couldn't show any signs of weakness. He didn't like their odds of surviving this situation.

"How do we know we'll live after we tell you anything?" Young Mack asked with venom lacing his voice.

"If I wanted you dead, you'd be dead already. You got caught slipping and didn't even realize how bad you were slipping, but we all know that slippers count, now tell me where the money is."

"The money is inside my gym bag under the couch," Ashton surrendered his portion of the take for the sake of their safety. The intruders stooped low and eyed the gym bag before pulling out the almost weightless bag.

"This can't be all of it, where is the rest of it?" the lead guy stated with distaste.

"It's all w—" Ashton's lie got shoved back down his throat before he could even get it out.

"Uuuhhh," Ashton groaned from the blow of a shotgun to the face. He was in so much pain that he couldn't open his eyes if he wanted to. Young Mack seethed with a murderous rage and struggled against his restraints.

"Fuck you do that dumb shit for!" Rob yelled from underneath the dismantled door he was stuck under. The weight of several men kept him in place and unable to move.

"Shut the hell up!" The lead man quieted all the noise that came after that statement.

"That wasn't shit compared to what I'ma do to the next mufucka stupid enough to try to lie to me. Now run me the fuckin' money or not one of you leaves here alive."

"Look inside of the red hoodie on that old chair," Young Mack surrendered what he had for him and his pops. The guy in charge looked on as his men searched the red hoodie and smiled at the bundles of money clutched in their hands.

"That's what I'm talking about," the lead man said once all the money was dropped into his palms. He worshipped young hustlers like Young Mack and his crew of thieves. Their names had been ringing all across town as one of the best crews getting it and he couldn't wait for his chance to eat off of their hard work.

He'd been having them watched for over a month, and they never saw what was to come. Once his men told him the boys were up to something, his antennas went up and he began to plot. Now he was sitting pretty with their winnings in his hands and was ready to get outta there. He didn't care to kill the young men who had so much life to live; they were the least of his worries. Even if they figured out who he was, he knew no one would come for him in fear of dying.

"Well, gentlemen, it was nice kicking it with y'all," he said as he stood to leave. "Oh, and before I forget—thanks!" The crew of intruders burst into a fit of laughter and walked out, each taking a turn to stomp on the door that had Rob pinned to the floor.

Rob grunted after each man stomped over him on their way out the door. Young Mack fumed at the realization that someone was taking them for their hard earned money. He struggled to free himself from the hard plastic of the zip-ties around his wrist and ankles. His movements stopped the moment he heard footsteps reapproaching.

"Y'all got everything, man!" Rob called out while struggling to stand up straight. He was praying that his portion of the take wasn't about to get taken next.

"Yeah, I know," the intruder muttered before delivering a devastating blow to Rob's temple with the butt of his shotgun. The blow immediately knocked him unconscious. Young Mack knew that meant that he and Ashton were about to receive the same treatment, so he braced himself for the blow that would indeed put his lights out.

"Come on, man, you don't have to do all that," Ash spoke through a pair of swollen lips. Young Mack wasn't sure if Ashton had lost any teeth from the earlier blow, but his words didn't sound like they were coming from his mouth.

"Shut the fuck up!" the goon growled after slamming his weapon against Ashton's temple, knocking him out. Young Mack looked on as the goon made his way over to him. His heart began pounding against his chest so hard he thought it would jump outta his body and make a dash for it. The man stood over him and watched as he tried to steady his breathing. He almost felt sorry for having to do them this way, but he knew how his boss moved and didn't feel remorse for anything they did to eat.

"Sorry, lil' man, I gotta do what I get paid to do, you feel me?" the man said before slamming his weapon into Young Mack's head. Young Mack wanted to yell out in pain. His eyes blurred, and he felt the heat of his own blood seeping outta his head. Everything seemed to slow down as he began to fade out, but it was then that he heard someone else enter.

"Phatts said hurry yo ass up before we leave without you, Skooby!"

"Man, shut the fuck up before I whack you with this mufucka next."

Young Mack heard the dreadful name that no one wanted to hear in a situation like this. He was glad to still be alive after hearing that. He flashed back to the many times he'd heard that name outta fear, growing up in the hood. The pain from the blow was overwhelming and he began to lose consciousness. After visualizing Phatts there staring down on them, daring them to challenge him, his world went black.

"Fuck!"

Chapter Two

"This can't be life," Young Mack sighed as he submitted to a pat down search after arriving at USP Atlanta. He knew the drill way too well and couldn't imagine what it was like for the guys on the inside trying to make it down to see their loved ones for a visit. He shook his head at the thought of ever being locked behind the walls that separated the incarcerated and their freedom. Not Young Mack; he couldn't allow that to happen. He hated the police, and the thought of the crooked ass court and prison systems made his stomach turn. Young Mack wasn't the rawest of street cats but he swore to hold his down in the streets, fuck prison!

"Who are you here to see?" a burly looking white man in a prison cop uniform asked him without taking his eyes from the computer screen before him. Young Mack immediately disliked the guy behind the computer because he had zero tolerance for disrespect, and talking to a man without looking him in the eyes was definitely a sign of disrespect.

"I'm here to see Mackentosh Miller," Young Mack stated with pride, as if the officer should've recognized it from his face. Young Mack and his father shared their features as if they were twins.

From the moment he mentioned his father's name the guard instantly wore a sour expression and it pissed Young Mack off. Young Mack exercised patience and shook the dirty looks from the Stone Cold Steve Austin lookalike.

"Bitch ass red neck!" Young Mack mumbled under his breath as the officer gave him a visitor's pass and allowed him to move along behind the other visitors. He took another look at the officer and their eyes met, right then he made a mental note to ask his father about the crooked looking guard.

The door to the visitation area swung open, and families filed out as others hurried to enter and visit their loved ones. Young Mack took his time, knowing the wait before his pops would be a bit longer than the others. He took the free time to gather them something to snack on while sharing this time together. He grabbed a couple of ham and cheese hot pockets and a bag of sour cream and onion, *Lays* chips for himself. He grabbed them both something to drink, added all types of snacks for his father who never seemed to eat, then handed everything for his father to the officers assigned to watch over the visitation area. The officers thoroughly inspected the food without contaminating it, then handed it back to him and let him proceed to the area assigned to him and his father for visit.

The entire visitation room acknowledged when Mackentosh 'Mr Mackmillions' Miller came into view. His confident GQ swagger was something to either deal with or simply just close your eyes. He demanded attention from everywhere, and eyes roamed from all over trying to get a look at what a magnificent creation he was. Young Mack smiled as his father approached their table. Even in his starched down khaki two piece, Mr. Mackmillions still carried himself as if he were draped in his usual high-end fabrics off the shelves of Saks Fifth or Bloomingdales. Young Mack was definitely his father's son when it came to designer staples. His Robin Jeans were cut and bleach-stained like those of the many A-list rappers he often saw rocking the pricey threads. His fitted Gucci-printed polo top gripped his athletic frame like a glove on a surgeon's hand. His father smiled and praised him for his sense of style. He especially took a liking to the Italian-made Gucci loafers that adorned his son's feet. Mr. Mackmillions had always had a fancy for the foreign brand.

"Good to see you young cats have a little flava. Son, you look good," Mr. Mackmillions said while embracing his only child.

22

"I see you ain't letting these crackers stop yo shine none, you looking good too. And what's with the guns, man?" Young Mack wasn't truly surprised by his father's firmness, he was naturally a strong man both in mind and body.

"Yeah, I gotta keep up with the younger pimps in this place. I'm Mr. Mackmillions, baby. I can't let 'em outshine me, not even on my worst day."

They shared a hearty laugh at the sound of that. Young Mack always felt good being around his father. He always found a way to keep Young Mack in a good mood.

"Pops, what's good with that wrestler look-alike up front?" Young Mack needed to know.

"Who? Grimes? That ol' gambling junkie. He'd bet his dick off of his body if he could." They both laughed at that. "Has he been giving you a hard time?"

"Naw, just hard stares that make me wanna punch his silly ass to death." Young Mack hated the way that officer looked at him after hearing his father's name.

"Don't sweat him, he's probably just mad that his Patriots lost to my Eagles and set his ass back ten large." They shared a laugh, being that Mr. Mackmillions made sure that his son made the same bet.

"Anyway, since we have the time to talk, what's up with the cookies from the last picknick? Red told me that the weather was bad, so spill it." Young Mack loathed the embarrassment of their last job. It had been weeks and he still wasn't over the sting of becoming prey to a much cleverer predator. The fuel to the fire was the fact that he'd never let his father down before, and now he had to explain how he and his crew got robbed for their winnings.

Mr. Mackmillions felt his son's mood change and the thick silence that followed just didn't seem right; he knew something was wrong but he just didn't know what.

"Look, son, I saw the news so I know the take went well. Now you need to tell me what I'm not aware of."

"Fuck it, ain't no way to sugar-coat it! We got took at the spot, Pop, right after we broke bread." Young Mack confessed.

"Got took?" Mr. Mackmillions was furious, his voice barely above a whisper. He couldn't believe the shit coming outta his son's mouth right now. It was the last thing he expected to hear him say. Who would be crazy enough to violate his name by touching Young Mack. Someone was definitely gonna pay for that!

"It was like the niggas was sitting on us or some shit, Pop. At first, I assumed there was a foul on the home team, but the way these clowns came at us—it was clear that they had planned on doing that for a while. They were dressed in HPD jackets with detective badges around their necks."

Lowering his voice to a whisper, Young Mack went on: "Came in and flipped the spot upside down while they zip-tied me and my crew. I thought we were being arrested, especially after what happened with those squad cars."

"Yeah, I saw that," Mr. Mackmillions stated.

"Good because that's another issue we need to discuss. Without bodies getting dropped I knew it wasn't the real boys in blue coming at us. We lost both our shares and the lil' homie Ash lost his too."

"What about the other cat, what's his name?"

"Rob."

"Yeah, what's up with him?" Mr. Mackmillions was looking at it from all angles. He was from the old school and could spot a flaw in the game from a mile away.

"Don't worry, Pop, he's official. He split his cut as close to the middle as he could. Gave us twelve apiece and kept fourteen for himself. I'll take Red your bread as soon as I make it back in town. Just wanted to let you know what was going on before I made it that way."

"Okay, that's cool. Do we have any leads on who hit y'all?" Mr. Mackmillions asked, already plotting their deaths.

"We don't need any leads, someone slipped up and said the name of the person who came at us." Young Mack stated. He could see how surprised his father was by that news.

"Run it."

"Phatts."

At the mention of the name, Mr. Mackmillions' mind drifted from the visitation room and traveled back to a time when Phatts was making a name for himself in the game. It was back in 1985 when he first heard the name Phatts spoken about and the mention of his loyal crew of outlaws. They were a younger generation and were always defying the laws of the land. Nothing or no one around wanted a piece of what Phatts and his henchmen had to offer.

Mr. Mackmillions was cut from a different cloth and a sport in every aspect of the word. He was the big fish in the pond, and Phatts knew all about the infamous Mackentosh Miller, and Mr. Mackmillions was quickly learning about him as news rained in raw and uncut. Neither legend feared the other, not in the least bit. Mr. Mackmillions felt superior and with good reasoning, definitely because he was a cut above the rest of the downed players that felt Phatts wrath. Those men were weak and couldn't hold a torch to Mr. Mackmillions; he knew it and so did they. Most of them came to him for encouragement to go up against their feared rival.

Thinking back, their first run-in was on neutral grounds at the National Player's Ball in 1988. Every hustler, mover, shaker and titan of the underworld came out for the legendary event. Mr. Mackmillions and his crew, along with their henchmen, were a sight for everyone's eyes. He was never to be out done by any man walking the face of the earth. That was the way he viewed it and carried himself with an air of sophistication. Nothing he did was on an average scale, and he was definitely the top dog of his era and loved every minute of it.

Respect was demanded and shown back all the same when it came to Mackentosh Miller. His rep was known by all, and no one dared disrespect him unless they were prepared to go to war or were flat-out ready to get found inside a grocery store's dumpster. Mr. Mackmillions mentally held a certain level of respect for the name, Phatts. He was prepared for whenever the stars aligned and brought them into the same setting together. Just as Lady Luck would have it, *The Player's Ball* would be their very first night setting eyes on each other.

"Well, if the wind ain't thin and the earth ain't flat, I know one thing for certain, this man has to be Mr. Mack!" Mr. Mackmillions remembered the stylish and precise man saying. Phatts wore minimum jewelry during his day-to-day, but on the night of the ball he was dressed to the nines and covered in expensive diamonds with thick gold chains and rings.

Mr. Mackmillions smiled at the sight of the man before him. His date was a beauty that Mackmillions had had his eyes on for the better half of a year. He then understood why she chose to play hard ball after seeing her on the arm of such an upcoming legend in the streets. Seeing Mr. Mackmillions out and about and with the power he exuded while many bowed in his presence made her panties moist. He was definitely the shit in her eyes.

"That be me," Mackmillions remembered himself, nodding and kissing the right hand of the beauty on Phatts' arm. He took Phatt's hand in his and shook it as well.

"What you know good, Phatts?" he stated, affirming that he too did his homework and knew who he was.

"I can't call it, big man," Phatts smiled, appreciating being known by such a sporting figure in the game.

That night everything progressed positively. Mr. Mackmillions actually enjoyed peeping into the mind of the man who put so much fear into the hearts of his many peers and business associates alike. Looking back at it, he couldn't help but like the guy and admire his courage to take on the streets. The young man was a lion, true-to-form, in a jungle where he had rights to consume anything he deemed lesser than he, especially if the other predators allowed him to.

It was that very night that a bond was made between two street juggernauts. It was that very night replaying in Mr. Mackmillions' mind as he made his way back to his cell block. Passers-by could feel the heat radiating off the normally chilled and charismatic Mackentosh Miller. Most spoke outta respect, but kept kicking after slight head nods from Mr. Mack. By the time he reached his pod, steam could be seen coming from his head; he was that heated. Sweat beaded his perfectly lined mustache as he entered his cell from the dayroom. After realizing his cellmate was out, probably working the trash crew, he quickly covered his cell door, retrieved the tool from the cell vent and went to work.

Five minutes later, he was putting everything into place to power up his Galaxy phone. Dialing a number from memory, he waited patiently for the line to go live.

"Yo, Mack man, what's up?" Jack joyfully answered, happy to hear from his lifelong friend.

"I need you to link me through to someone," Mr. Mackmillions spoke sharply.

"You say it and it's done." Jack replied dead ass.

"I need a scheduled talk with Phatts."

"Phatts? Are you sure you want me to link that up while you are still on the inside?" Jack questioned. He was one of Mack's loyal friends and believed everyday could be the day that he graced the outside world again.

"Definitely," Mr. Mackmillions confirmed.

"Cool. Just give me twenty-four hours to make some necessary calls, and hit me back. If I don't answer, then you know what his response was."

"Twenty-four hours exactly," Mr. Mack concluded their call.

Shortly after his call with Jack, he made himself a hot cup of coffee and sat down on his bunk and thought about the person he was about to call. Their bond was air-tight and it had been a while since he last reached out, but he needed to make this call for sure.

The line went live after the third ring, and he came face to face with the woman he trusted with his life and soul thereafter.

"It's about time you rung this old line," she smiled her beautifully bright-toothed smile. She loved admiring his handsome face every time they *Skyped* with one another. It was like time was against everything on earth besides him, and she loved seeing his face light up.

"Em, I need you, Babykakes," he said as he too admired her gorgeous features. Her green eyes and full painted lips were a sight for any man's pleasure.

"I'm sure you do, isn't that the only time you call—"

"Another time for that, love," he cut her off.

"It's Lil' Mack, isn't it?" she rebounded quickly, knowing he would never purposely disrespect her like that.

"Yeah, we have a problem and I need your help to fix it."

"Talk to me, tell me what I need to be doing." She listened intently at everything he needed for her to do.

"I'll get straight on it and be there to see you soon with results," Em promised. He called out to her before the line went dead on him.

"Yeah?"

"Thank you," he smiled.

28

"You're welcome," she replied and returned his smile.

"Alright, ma, be careful because this could get dangerous," he warned.

"Don't much worry about me, I can take care of myself."

"I believe you," he smiled and said goodbye before their call ended.

He sat there on his bunk thinking of ways to make Phatts suffer for laying hands on his seed. It was against everything they had in place, but if he wanted to buck, shit was 'bout to get real for him if Mr. Mackmillions had something to say about it. He took his time dismantling his phone and putting it back in the cell's stash spot before lying down in bed and staring at nothing in particular. He couldn't wait to get the ball rolling with his appeal because his son needed him, and it hurt him deep down knowing he couldn't be there in the ways he wished he could. But the streets were gonna be in surprise when he actually broke the chain and graced the ground once again, and this time he promised himself to make it worth every second he spent behind bars.

Chapter Three

"A fuckin' wall! Young, have you heard what this stupid mu'fucka is proposing?" Deuce was heated after watching Fox News and the president of the United States was preparing to build a wall around the Texas-Mexico border.

"Yeah, dude a real dick," Young Mack uttered as he stepped past Deuce who was sitting on the living room sofa watching their eighty-two inch QLED TV.

"What's good? You sound like someone killed your favorite dog or sum' shit."

"You know I don't mix my hustles, bruh. You my nigga one hunid grand, but my stresses on the other side cannot become your stresses. Pops always taught me to separate my business ventures that way." Young Mack couldn't put the words together to explain how he felt. After visiting his father, he was even more troubled than he was before he went in.

"Alright, cool, homey, I can respect that," Deuce said, killing the power on the TV screen. "So what's it looking like for the home team? I know shit 'bout to get brazy if this idiot gets this wall up." He couldn't stand the taste of the words coming out of his own mouth due to the president's actions towards immigration and the war against terrorist cells. At least that's what he wants the world to think. Who knows what they're up to!

"Shit still on the up for us for now. I just copped so we're good for a while but I will be checking on that asap." He really wasn't sure how things were gonna play out once his coke connect caught wind of this multi-billion-dollar project the president was requesting. "Call Chris and Hog, tell 'em get here pronto, we got work to do!" Deuce smiled when he heard those words thrown over Young Mack's shoulder as he made his way to the back of the trap house.

Watch how I break my wrist / Make that water whip / Stretch it out, then flip / I'm all about my chips / I get it out the mud / Turn up in 2 seconds—

Chris could hear the music blasting from the kitchen the moment he and Hog stepped through the front door of the trap. It was a spot they shared with Young Mack and Deuce, so they all had keys to it.

"What the fuck, ock?" Deuce stopped what he was doing once the music shut off.

"What I tell y'all about bumping this new wave shit when you doing old-school work?" Chris smiled. He was the least bit worried about his young homey's attitude. These were his guys, his pupils in the cook game. It was he who schooled them in the art of cooking up crack cocaine. It was Young Mack who paid their way through it but eventually, Chris came to love the ambitious duo and gave them the game on how to stretch and mix the potent coke Young Mack's supplier was coming through with, enough to add tens of thousands to Young Mack's profit margin.

Chris began to bop his head to the sounds of the late great Pimp C of the Texas rap group, *The Underground Kings,* as it erupted through the Beats Pill speakers set up around the kitchen at every station.

"*I bought my first key from my big momma's brother—*" They all rapped along while busying themselves with their task of cooking the full three bricks Young Mack had brought out for them to distribute to his trap houses and workers around the hood.

After hours in the lab, Chris was still hyped and the fellas loved his energy. Chris was an OG to the game and made sure of them staying on top of their game.

"You see why I jams out to that old-school crack music!" he said, holding up a Ziploc bag full of yellowish crack (*cookies* is what the streets called them) ounces.

"That new wave shit is for that new wave dope. Old school shit is for the purer and quality-tested product," Chris went on.

"Man, we just spent hours in there whipping our asses off, so what are you talkin' about *purer?*" Deuce laughed.

"Naw, young buck, what you was in there doing was adding a mixture of baking soda and just enough water to hydrate the product. The only way to do that is to melt it down, turn your fork a lil' bit to combine for one helluva Chris crack cross!" Chris burst into a fit of laughter at his reference to the old hip-hop group *Kriss Gross.*

They all knew hands down that he was the best cook in their area and possibly the entire city when it came to his skills. It was the very reason Young Mack chose him to be their mentor, along with a little push from his father to hit him up.

"No, seriously though. Too many pops of that there fork and the wrong timing will set your product back on the smoker's pipe scale. Stay consistent with the method. You can always add to it as you grow, but never take away from it if you wanna remain relevant in this crack world." Chris jeweled them.

"You know we appreciate the knowledge, old head, and you have my word that we won't be switching this shit up. Why fuck up something so perfect? Naw, we ain't on that type of shit!" Young Mack said.

"No problem, youngin," Chris replied as he stashed his cut of their hard work inside of his G-Star hoodie. "Hey, have y'all heard what our ignorant ass president been talkin' about?"

"Yeah, we heard about it, what's the plan, Young," Hog spoke up. He was the quietest of the group, but surely the deadliest.

Young Mack took a liking to the younger hustler shortly after hooking up with Chris. Hog lived in the shadows. Due to Chris getting up in age, he always needed a savage around him that wouldn't hesitate to blow a nigga's shit off his shoulders, and Hog was that and more because he hustled to keep himself fed as well. Hog loved his position in the crew and he loved them all like brothers, especially Young Mack. The thrill of being around someone not that much older than him, but lived the life of a man twice their age was alluring. It was what Deuce loved about being a part of their crew also. Together, Hog and Deuce shared the power behind the push while earning their keep and remaining loyal to men of loyalty. It was enthusiastic to them.

"As of now shit still the same until I get word otherwise, but like I mentioned to Deuce earlier, I just copped so we should be good for as long as we're good, ya feel me," Young Mack replied as best as he could. Truth was he didn't know where they stood and wouldn't know until he got with his people.

"Just keep us informed as best as you can, young homey," Chris understood his situation all too well. "I'm out."

"Yeah, me too," Young Mack said after collecting enough bags to supply his field soldiers and the crack houses he had set up all over. "I'll hit you once my route is covered."

"Loyalty," Deuce stated while slapping hands with Young Mack before Young Mack left the spot.

The AMG C63 S, Mercedes Benz lit the eyes of every hustler and gold digger Young Mack cruised past on the way to his trap locations. It was a little something he gifted himself. Of course, like everything else, it was in his mother's name. The streets were loving it just like he thought they would.

"What's poppin', Young Mack!"

"Hey, handsome!"

"These streets belong to you now, Young Mack!" People yelled out to him and he took it all in stride with slight nods of his head as people spoke. He loved the fact that it was him that everyone was acknowledging, his name meant something now.

For years everyone recognized him as his father's son and no one knew anything about the distinct factor hidden inside of the legacy left behind for his dwelling. Now he had his own reputation and he was enjoying the attention that came along with it.

As he rounded the block on Delano and Tuam Avenue, he saw the fiends lined up the block in the cool of the day. Fall provided the best weather in the hood for their kind of hype, and the smokers were out in droves. Young Mack looked up the block and down the other end before stepping outta his whip, two large Ziploc bags on deck, concealed from the world's eye view. Before parking, he swept the block and its surrounding blocks to check with the cluckas they had on payroll to make sure the streets were clear of cops and, more importantly, robbers.

The rural gravel driveway doubled as a parking lot for the small set of apartment units where he structured his compound for crack sells. As he made his way to the door where his head lieutenant operated out of, he saw smokers clinging to the shadows between each unit. It provided the perfect covers from the street and there were nice havens where they could blaze and shop without having to ever leave the spot. But as nice as it was to a hustla with enough work to keep them there, Young Mack didn't like the smokers hanging around their place of business.

Young Mack used his signature knock once he made it to the front door and the door was snatched open in haste. There stood his diamond-toothed protégé looking at him as

34

if he was Christmas itself. He could hear the sounds of Kevin Gates 'Money Long' playing on the inside.

"What's the bidness, big bruh?" Pooh yelled. Seeing his big homey at the door only meant one or two things and he knew what this visit meant for sure, and he was hyped as hell.

"What's with all these heads cluckin' around here like they running this spot, or am I confused and they do run this spot and y'all the ones cluckin' around!" Young Mack scolded his soldier and his counterparts, ignoring his greeting. Pooh stared at his mentor and friend as if he was crazy for leaving him hanging.

"Shit, we been cluckin' around here waiting' on yo ass for over eight hours without product, bruh! So if we waiting on you, who the hell you think they waiting on?" Pooh stood up for himself without flinching one bit. Young Mack instantly felt bad for blasting off on his loyal protégé like that.

"My bad, gee! A nigga just been hella busy and hella stressed, ya feel me." He apologized and gave his young homey some love before apologizing to the rest of the crew.

"Okay, big bruh! Now what you brought for us?" Pooh exclaimed while rubbing his palms together. He knew the huge bulge under Young Mack's hoodie was the packs for him and his team to get it on. The smokers were about to rejoice and praise their team once he stepped out to serve them.

"You already know I came to get y'all right."

"That's that cray right there, ain't it!" Pooh asked after taking the two bags filled with crack cookies.

"Mos def," Young Mack laughed at his boy.

"Okay, bool. Lil' Mat, grab that bread for big bruh! Rat, get the yaapa, throw me my yat and let's get out here and get to this yeapa!" Pooh was one fearless lieutenant and ran things well within his crew of savages. Young Mack smiled as he watched him take charge and lead his team. He sat down and grabbed up the remote control to the PS4 and played a game of *Madden* while he waited for Lil' Mat to finish his count.

The sun slowly peeped over the thick grey clouds as Young Mack made his way to his other trap houses. He bopped his head to music as he turned the corner from Tuam Avenue, making a left on Canfield Street. Canfield was always a lit spot to do business all day and night long, and Young Mack loved when his homey found a solid location to get money and remain outta sight and outta mind from the authorities.

Women waved and blew kisses at the young hustla as he drove the block. He stopped and parked his Benz across from a legendary club that no longer existed. Looking across the street at the old familiar lot, a thought of opening another club there ran across his mind. He nodded at the idea of doing just that. Eyes were on him before his Italian-made loafers touched the concrete. He gave his man a nod from ways away once their eyes landed on each other.

"What's good, my little big homey?" K-dawg laughed as he accepted a pound from Young Mack. K-dawg was a beast, standing at a statued six foot five inches with two hundred and forty pounds of toned muscles. His heavily tatted frame added to the already intimidating allure of his monstrous size and rep in the street. Dude was about his get down for sure.

"Why yo big ass ain't never got a shirt on?" Young Mack said as he admired the candy red '64 Impala he was sitting on. The wheels on the car were the perfect blend of black with a thin line of white and a thin line of yellow. The wired rims stuck out longer than a giraffe's neck and sparkled as the day brightened.

"Look at me, would you ever wear a shirt and cover up all this gangsta if you were me?" K-dawg burst into a fit of laughter. Young Mack couldn't hate on his boy because dude was a beast compared to many, but he wasn't about to feed into his ego trip.

"What's good, bruh? You ready for me or what?" Young Mack asked after looking around inside the Chevy.

"What type of question is that when you know you running late as hell!" K-dawg frowned.

"Damn, I forgot. Plus yo spot stay hittin like that."

"And some, but that's just how shit is down here in the bottom. Los Ward been coming around coppin' and they wishing you would spread yo wings a bit and fuck with the niggas. You know they hard as fuck over there and the money will never be a problem with them, they eat greedy for real," K-dawg vouched.

"I understand, but it's a lot going on right now so I'll have to get back with you on that. But, what I will do is start doubling your package on this end so you can give them better numbers when they come through, and that's just outta love. You can let them know I ain't never turning them down but it's about to be some shit with them Mexicans and the government and we got to wait that storm out." K-dawg nodded his understanding.

He moved off the hood of his whip and started for the back of his spot with Young Mack closing in on his heels. He stepped to the trap's circuit box and snatched it open so that Young Mack could collect the bands of money hidden inside and replace it with the product he'd brought for him. Young Mack picked up and delivered just as he always did and left with a promise to double K-dawg's package before the end of the day. As he walked back to his vehicle, his phone erupted in his pocket.

"Hey, gorgeous, I was just thinking about seeing you," Young Mack answered, knowing Ambrea would cling to his every word.

"Well, why don't you make your way home and I'll meet you there on my lunch break?" Ambrea gushed.

"No doubt, ma, I'm there!"

"I'll see you there in about twenty minutes then, right?"

"Absolutely, but don't forget the chocolate." His dick throbbed, thinking about her sexy ass wetting his shit with her super soaker pussy.

"You's a true freak, you know that," she laughed, feeling her middle dampen her lace panties. Thinking of him expertly stroking her deep had her head in the clouds.

"Only for you, baby girl, now hurry yo ass up!" Young Mack said, ending their call.

Young Mack made it home in no time and was surprised to see Ambrea already there. Her car was parked outside of his condo. He smiled thinking of how horny he must have made her over the phone for her to beat him there. He used his key to unlock the security gate at the entrance of the building and hurried through the front door.

"Baby—Ssss—hurry up, I need you." He swallowed a chuckle, realizing that she had begun without him.

The sight of her flawless honey-toned, sun-kissed skin made his mouth water as his dick stiffened to full potential. Her naked body was like a work of art due to the countless hours she spent in the gym keeping her body tight. He quickly stripped himself outta his clothes and watched her closely. The chocolate syrup sat on the nightstand next to where she lay; he grabbed it and joined her on his king-size bed.

"I see you couldn't wait for me, huh?" Young Mack said as he drizzled chocolate all over her breasts, down her six- packed torso to her freshly waxed pussy. The cold sensation of the liquid on her skin ignited something inside of her as it slowly spread over her body, sending her over the edge before his tongue ever touched her body. She was loving it and needing him even more now.

"You're gonna have me all sticky at work now," she purred between sobs of pleasure as her orgasm settled.

He put his hand on top of hers and took over where she'd left off. "Naw, ma, I'm 'bout to lick yo sexy ass clean!"

Young Mack meant every word, and her moans heightened his efforts as he explored her breasts with his expert tongue, playing close attention to her sensitive gumdrop sized nipples. He knew he loved when he manipulated her breasts, often bringing her to climax from that stimulation alone. He often thought that her nipples had a direct connection to the G-spot in her pussy and he knew just how to work them.

"Ohhh shit!" she moaned, as another climax propelled her to the next level.

Young Mack savored the mixture of her juices and the rich chocolate off her body. His plan was to tease her but the vibrations of her body made him hungry for her soaked pussy. She cried out from the ever mounting pleasure of his tongue and fingers manipulating the spot only he knew existed.

"Damn, babe, eat that shit, oooo—Oh my gawd! That feels good!" Just as her climax reached heights of never before experience, he slipped his hardness inside and drove all the way in with ease. The wetness from her climaxes propelled his way through and through.

"Whose pussy is this?" Young Mack boasted as her legs squeezed his body close. He pulled himself out until only the tip of his hardness remained inside before plunging all inches back inside of her. The sensation of his rod connecting with her spot over and over had her coming time and time again as he chased one of his own. He slowed his strokes in order to hold out just a while longer.

"Ass up, face down!" he ordered as he watched her juices drip from his dick like he'd never seen before. She quickly obliged his order and waited impatiently as he admired her from the back.

Young Mack reached for his jeans and removed the surprise he had bought for this occasion. He rubbed his dick between her puffy wet lips and did the same with her surprise before pressing it gently between her spread ass cheeks.

"Sssss—ohhhh shit, baby, I love you," she hissed while climaxing yet again instantly after the toy slid through her tight sphincter. The pain hurt so good once he filled her empty pussy and proceeded to pound her from the back until he spilled his heavy load deep inside of her. She exploded again from the euphoria of being double-penetrated, mixed with the pressure of his seeds soaring through her womb.

"I think I better call in sick," she smiled seductively after regaining her thoughts and body functions. Young Mack laughed and tapped her on the ass before standing from the bed.

"And don't remove that plug until I tell you to." He laughed at her gap-legged walk as he followed behind her to the bathroom.

"Freak!" Ambrea couldn't contain the satisfied smile on her face. She was enjoying the toy being there. So much so she bent all the way over as she adjusted the water temperature, purposely giving him an unobstructed view of her pretty pussy and the toy stuffed inside of her ass. She could feel a stir in both places as he stood behind her, stroking himself back to life. Right then he decided that he had to have her once more before she left for work.

"Do you ever get enough of doing this to me?" She laughed as he approached and pulled her to him by her small waist.

"Hell no!" he replied, then entered her wetness roughly from behind.

Chapter Four

Rob sat in the back of the stolen minivan stressing over all the things he needed to get done, but had no money to get it done with. Life was throwing all types of challenges his way, and he hadn't heard a word from Young Mack about their next job. Shit was tight on his end, his pockets were empty and he couldn't take it any longer.

"What's the order, kid? Are we just gonna sit here lookin' at the damn building or we 'bout to get out and handle up?" Rob was tired of waiting on the others he'd joined on a desperate caper in an attempt to put some paper in his pockets. He was even more tired of being broke and on his ass.

"Yeah, what the fuck is we waitin' fa'?" Max asked. He was unlike Virgil and was always hyped about putting in work. The thrill of a score is what kept his days lively.

"We gotta be sure that the manager is on deck, she's the only one that'll have the code to the safe!" Virgil stated, wishing the others would chill and let him do what he did best, or so he thought.

"Bruh, this is a business, not a trap, so I'm pretty sure they have shifts and different cards. You've been watching this joint for weeks, right?" Rob asked as Virgil turned in his seat; his eyes were full of frustration.

"Yeah, why?"

"Have you ever known the manager to have off days?" Rob asked, now getting frustrated himself for riding out with such local jokers in the take game.

"Yeah, her off days are Mondays and Tue—oh shit, I'm trippin'—today is Tuesday, so that means we gotta look out for a fat white guy who has crazy acne—"

"Let me guess," Rob cut him off mid-sentence.

"This guy should be wearing a red Polo top and carrying a small duffle." Virgil looked into Rob's eyes, wondering how he could possibly know details on this caper that he'd scoped alone. Rob could see the question in his eyes and shook his head at how clumsy this dude really was.

"Saw dude over half an hour ago, so we sittin' out this bitch with all this heat for nuthin'," Rob stated, then sat back exhausted from dealing with this clown.

"Fuck it, let's do what we came to do," Max stated and was halfway outta the sliding door of the van before Virgil spoke against it.

"Kill all that, Max, let's rock, grab that carry bag." Rob was no longer tryna hear Virgil's whims about leaving the job. They'd spent the better half of an hour waiting on a person that was never gonna show because of him, and now he wanted to abandon the mission. Rob was hungry and Max was down for the play, so they entered the building with just the two of them.

"Everybody on the floor, now!" Max yelled out and got everyone's attention. After seeing the automatic weapon in his hands, no one wanted anything to do with him and complied immediately.

"Face down! Nobody looks up, nobody gets hurt. If I see your eyes, you might as well say the Lord's Prayer because I ain't hesitating to end you!" Rob stated as he stepped over customers on his way behind the counter where the manager was.

"You, fat boy—red shirt, get up and open this safe. Don't try to be a hero, this money is insured so just unlock the safe and we'll be on our way. Don't make me have to use one of these innocent people lying in here to get you to comply because I definitely will," Rob swore and the guy didn't hesitate to do as he instructed.

To his dislike they'd have to wait five minutes for the safe to open, something Virgil never brought to their attention. Once again, he punched himself for dealing with that clown. At least Max was down to get his hands dirty and Rob commended him for that, but this guy Virgil was playing with his freedom and his livelihood.

The next five minutes was the longest five minutes of his life, and he was starting to feel bad about the entire job, that was until they heard the loud ding from the safe's timer go off.

"About damn time," Rob sighed before stepping over to the safe and opening its door. "What the fu—" His jaw hit the floor, leaving his mouth gapped wide as he stared into the nearly empty safe.

He ran his hands through the empty shelves just to be sure that he wasn't losing his damn mind and seeing things. He cursed Virgil silently as he took out the money that was there for them and promised to make him pay for his ignorance and wasting his time.

"Let's get outta here," Rob told Max as he passed him on his way out the door.

They rode in silence the entire way back to Max's crib. Rob was desperately battling his demons and the thoughts they were giving him of killing Virgil for the shitty job he'd done casing the place they'd just robbed. Max knew something was wrong once he saw Rob emerge from behind the counter with a nearly deflated bag. There couldn't have been more than a few grand in there the way that Rob was carrying it, and the look in his eyes confirmed it and let him know that shit was about to hit the fan.

"So what's the split?" Virgil asked as they sat inside of Max's kitchen at an old wooden table made for dining.

"You said that you've been watching that place for weeks, right?" Rob asked Virgil without looking at him.

"You asked me that already and my answer is the same."

"Did you know that the safe had a timer on it? No, never mind that question, did you ever step foot inside of that fuckin' place at all?" Rob yelled, and spittle flew from his mouth.

"Whooa, calm down, my nigga, I ain't the one to be—" Virgil's words were cut short by the huge right hook Rob landed, connecting with his jaw.

"Arrgh, bitch ass nigga, you snuck me!" Virgil groaned as he tried to get his vision straight, but Rob wasn't for it.

"You stupid dick, you could've gotten us knocked!" Rob yelled as he delivered blow after blow until Virgil finally fell to the floor in pain. Rob proceeded in stomping his ass out with his butter-wheat Timbs.

Rob must have stomped and kicked Virgil until his ass ran outta breath. He was heated and had every reason to be, but as much as he hated Virgil at that moment, he hated himself for going against his promise to stick with Young Mack and Ash on every job and rocking with Virgil in the first place. While doing his best shit on the prick below his foot, he thought about how much he hated Young Mack for not showing up or at least having the decency to answer his calls.

Max just sat there smoking what was left of his pcp-dipped kush blunt as Rob maxed Virgil out; he didn't say a word. He watched the whole fiasco and understood Rob's anger.

"Yo, Max, split that shit in two so I can be out before I change my mind about killin' this clown," Rob spoke through labored breathing.

"I-I didn't-know," Virgil spoke and pain exploded in his rib cage. "Arrgh, fuck! My ribs!"

"Fuck yo ribs, nigga, I should wig yo silly ass for wasting my time and risking my freedom." Max shook his head once he did their count.

"Sixteen twenty-five apiece, you 'eard me," Max stated in his southern Louisiana drool.

"Waste of fuckin' time, yo, I'm out!" Rob grabbed his portion and bounced.

He couldn't believe the shit he'd just been a part of. He needed to find Young Mack and pull in some serious cash before he ended up doing some other dumb shit and winded up behind bars; he hated that thought alone and decided to call up Ash.

"Man, where the hell is Young Mack?" Rob asked once he had Ashton on the line.

"Shit, your guess is better than mine," Ash replied.

Rob had been calling around for weeks tryna get a hold of Young Mack. A month had passed since their last job got ruined by a team of jackers lying in wait for them to successfully pull it off, and Rob was losing his mind in hunger. He didn't have the type of fall back money as Young Mack and maybe even Ash, and he was out in the streets making bad moves and struggling to make ends meet.

"What the fuck is his problem? No lie, homey, this no call no show shit is getting played the fuck out!" Rob unleashed his anger because Young Mack was getting on his nerves.

"I feel you," Ashton replied, not knowing what else to say to his boy. He'd felt the pressure of not bringing in his own money since they'd gotten hit too. Even though he considered his bread well spent, he knew all too well how Rob was feeling, but he had patience and knew Young Mack was only following his father's orders to fall back for a while.

"Where are you?" Rob asked, seething.

"At home, why? What's up?"

"I'm on my way, we gotta find this nigga and talk some damn sense into him 'cause shit gettin' real out in these streets and I can't go too much longer without gettin' a bag."

"A'ight! Pull up," Ash laughed, thinking about how shit would surely end if the two of them were to bump heads.

As angry as he was about Young Mack's disappearance, Rob was forced to brighten up at the sight of Ashton's twin sister. Boy, was she a knock out! And he had the biggest crush on her. She was dressed to kill in a designer Dior dress that hugged her body perfectly and stopped just above her knees. She reminded him so much of Kim K, and just seeing her made his mouth water.

"How you doin' this evenin', beautiful?" Rob crooned as he stepped outside of his tricked out 750i Beamer.

"I'm doing just fine, how about yourself?" she asked with a wonderful smile on her angelic face that drove him wild with desire.

"Well, I had a lot to complain about, but after seeing you I can't even remember what none of that was," he returned her smile with one of his own.

"I can always appreciate a compliment when I hear one, so thank you."

"No thanks needed, ma, you're absolutely gorgeous," Rob replied.

"Yeah, yeah, yeah, enough of all that, let's bounce," Ash cut into their conversation. He wasn't too fond of Rob macking game to his sister.

"It was nice seeing you again," Rob stated after Ashton got inside of his ride and shut the passenger door.

"Same here and you better take care of my brother, wouldn't want to have to hunt you down behind that one." Rob shook his head at the glorious sight of her walking towards her Lexus truck after talking with him. Her ass was one he could never forget even if he never saw her again in life.

"I gotta have me some of that," Rob said to himself as he climbed back behind the wheel of his ride.

"She's outta your league, so quit while you're ahead," Ashton warned as he busied himself with the screen of his iPhone.

"Tsk, yeah, right! Outta my league my ass, boy, I'm 'bout to be your next brother-in-law!" Rob laughed as he peeled outta the neighborhood.

"Just don't disrespect her when she shoots that ass down, and we won't have any problems," Ash warned him but this time he was looking him dead in the eyes.

"Damn, kid, you threatening me now?" Rob asked, still a bit amused by his cock-blocking skills.

"Never that, you know you my dude. Thing is, I'm willing to die behind her, but are you willing to kill or die if you can't have her," Ashton asked before giving his attention back to his phone.

Rob didn't take Ashton's words as disrespect or as a threat; he respected how he felt about his family. Plus, he normally got who he wanted, so it wasn't his style to disrespect a woman that might turn down his advances. The fact that Ashton's sister never shied away from his conversations told him there was a chance that he could once again get what he wanted. Rob let his mind wonder as he drove around from spot to spot looking for Young Mack.

"So this is the spot ol' dude told us to check out?" Rob asked as they pulled up to the shotgun styled wooden house on Dennis Street.

"Yeah but I don't see his car parked out here," Ash replied as he looked around the area for signs of Young Mack.

"They trappin' so his car could be somewhere else, come on, let's check it out!" Rob suggested before checking the clip in his .45 automatic handgun then slamming one in the head. Ashton shook his head at the sight of his weapon.

"Nawl, it ain't that type of party. If these are Mack's people, then they're our people as well. No threat, no heat, bro!" Rob felt that Ash was right, but it would make him more comfortable if he had his piece on him.

"No threat, no heat, or we can wait and catch him at a different time," Ash reiterated.

"No threat, no heat," Rob reluctantly agreed and slid his weapon under his seat. His head was on swivel as they approached the steps that led to the front door of the small house.

"Stop right there! Y'all don't look like smokers, neither one of you work for me, and y'all don't look like one time either, so I take it that y'all here tryna take sum'n!" Ash and Rob flinched hard after hearing the sound of a shotgun racking one in the chamber.

"Hold up, we're here lookin' for Young Mack, he's our people and we haven't seen him in weeks!" Rob yelled with his hands in the air, hoping whoever was on the other side of that door didn't pull the trigger.

Deuce calmed himself after hearing Young Mack's name, but even though they weren't a threat he still didn't know where Young Mack was at the moment. "Ain't no Young Mack at this address so I suggest y'all keep it movin' and I'll get word out that he's wanted."

"A'ight, cool with us!" Ashton said and hurried down the steps to catch up with Rob who was almost at the car.

"No threat, no heat, huh?" Rob laughed mockingly.

"That could've been anything behind that door, what was yo lil' gun gone do compared to that?" Ash laughed.

***

"Boss, we're waiting for your signal," Skooby spoke into his radio as he watched everyone get into position.

"Is everything in place?"

"Check," Skooby replied. He could see the entire area, and their men had it covered.

"In that case, go take sum'n!" Phatts sat idly and listened as the scene unfolded in the distance. Gunshots rang out, causing his adrenaline to spike. It had been some time now since his crew had had to put in some real work in the fields on their takes.

No time like the present, he thought to himself. He took a good pull from the cognac flavored cigar stuffed in the corner of his mouth and let out a big cloud of smoke before instructing his driver to let him out.

"Give me yo strap, AJ," Phatts ordered once his designer loafers touched the ground, followed by his signature marble finished walking cane.

"You got it, bossman," AJ replied as he surrendered his weapon.

"AJ, you been my driver for the better half of a decade, give or take, right?"

"Give or take," AJ agreed with an assuring smile.

"So why do you still call me that bossman shit. I consider you a dear friend of mine, very loyal and dear friend. I put my life in your hands everyday behind this wheel here and you protect it naturally, so from this day forward, AJ, call me Phatts just like everyone else."

"Sure thing, Phatts!" AJ smiled. Phatts didn't know what it was about this happy mu'fucka that made him keep the nigga around but he trusted him behind the wheel, and that's all that mattered to him.

"Now let me got tend to this bag," Phatts tilted his brim at his driver and moved past him.

Phatts was pleased with how precise and effective his men were. He looked around inside of the small disarrayed trap house and nodded at his men as he moved closer to his latest prey lying face down in a hog-tied position.

"See what you made Phatts do," he chuckled as he spoke of himself in third person while letting out a cloud of smoke. The sight of his prey's dead comrades in the same room did nothing to him as he looked over the reason he was there.

Phatts felt no pity nor remorse for the losers. He hated being stood up on his payments, and he dealt murderously with the ones that chose not to cough up his dough the same way he lent it out to them. Now he stood staring down on yet another nigga that felt like buckin' his system by missing his deadline.

"I told you not to make—it—come—to—this, didn't— I?" Phatts spoke in between kicks to his hog-tied victim's face and body.

"Come on, Phatts, you know I was gone make that right once I got it. Man, you jumping the gun!" Will coughed in agony.

"Missing your deadline wasn't a smart move whatsoever, mu'fucka and now I'm here to collect what's mine with interest."

"Whatever you say, man, just don't kill me, I got four mouths to feed." Will lied.

"Hell yeah, huh!" Phatts wasn't tryna hear none of that bull. He was there to get his paper and that alone. Who lived and died didn't much matter to him one bit. "Where is my money?"

Phatts chambered a round, making the tied man piss himself. Phatts and his entire crew burst into a fit of laughter from the big wet spot growing underneath him.

"The safe is under the floorboard in the back room's closet, just don't kill me." Will pleaded. He wasn't sure of what the turnout would be once they entered that room, but he prayed harder in that moment than he ever had in his entire life.

"What's the combo?" Skooby asked.

"Five-nine-twenty-thirteen. It's gonna take all y'all to get that shit outta there," he urged them.

"I'm sure my men can manage," Phatts confirmed with a nod to Skooby and the rest of their hit team.

Phatts sat and watched his prey once his men moved to the rear of the house. He was strongly considering letting Will live depending upon how much bread was really in that safe back there. Phatts nearly jumped outta his skin and his thoughts of freeing Will scrambled, as he landed behind the worn sofa he was once seated upon after automatic gun fire erupted in the back where his men were. He knew none of them had brought that type of artillery for this mission.

"The fucks goin' on back there?" Phatts asked himself while staying outta sight. He thought his men had cleared the house, but they obviously missed someone and he was now praying to make it outta there alive.

"Kill these muthafuckas, Rari! Make 'em bleed for this s—" Will's words were cut short the same as his life after Phatts fired three shots into the back of his head.

"Pussy ass mu'fucka! If any of my men are dead, I'ma kill yo bitch ass again!" Phatts was talking to the corpse of the dead man when he caught a glimpse of someone moving in his peripheral. He raised his weapon, ready to take a bitch nigga's life in a heartbeat, but calmed himself once Skooby announced himself. He held a black carry bag containing all that was inside of the safe, when he stepped to Phatts side and put two more into the head of Will for their lost men. It was as if he could read Phatts' brain.

"What the hell happened back there at the house?" Phatts asked Skooby as they rode in the back of his Bentley truck. Skooby remained speechless as he stared out at the world flying past them. Phatts didn't press him about it, but he knew his protégé would open up to him sooner rather than later.

"He had some young chick hidden in that closet, couldn't have been any older than eighteen years old. She got off a few rounds and killed Sam and Billy on impact, but she was too inexperienced to handle such a big weapon and its power threw her off balance. Once she fell, I felt joy in putting her down because she almost had us all back there.

We slipped big time and it nearly cost us all our lives!" Skooby explained.

"That doesn't explain why you lookin' like you really died back there," Phatts said as he thought to himself about how he would have been the last man standing had she killed all of his men in one sweep of her automatic weapon. He said this before tossing a few stacks into Skooby's lap.

"I hate killing women and children, Phatts!" The thought alone disgusted him.

"I can dig it, but we gotta eat out here or these mean ass streets will eat us alive, baby boy! This is how we eat, by any means necessary!" Phatts replied as he readied one of his cognac flavored cigars.

"That lil' bitch could have killed me and if it wasn't for this vest you talked me into wearing I'd surely be stankin' right now." Skooby shook his head at the sound of his own death.

"Don't mention it," Phatts stated, looking through their winnings. "AJ, take us to the club!"

Chapter Five

"Baby, be still!" Bianca growled for the third time since K-dawg had summoned her. She was stitching up the huge gash in the back of his head that he couldn't seem to tell her how he'd gotten.

"Gurl, you act like that shit don't supposed to hurt with yo heavy ass hands," K-dawg shot back.

He was mad as shit about the recent slip up because nothing had ever gotten by him like that before. Mad or not though, the needle she was pushing through his flesh was irritating the hell outta him.

K-dawg looked at this phone and saw that Young Mack still had not answered his messages or returned any of his phone calls, and he really needed to talk to his big homey. Death was around the corner for the bad hand someone had dealt him, and he needed his homey's blessing before he painted the city red. After gettin' his wound stitched up, he went by their trap spot to make sure the clean-up was done and everyone had moved out, before hitting Young Mack up again only to get the same results.

"Yo, big bruh, you gotta get at me before I lose my fuckin' marbles out here," he left a message on Young Mack's phone for the fourth time.

After leaving the trap spot and making sure everything was in line, K-dawg sat perched down the block from a very highly frequented liquor store, smoking some strong gas while watching out for the man he was sure would have some answers for him.

An hour passed before K-dawg spotted the man stepping inside of the liquor store. He checked his weapon and calmed himself as he approached the entrance of the liquor store. He needed answers and he was dead set on getting them.

The bell above the door chimed once he stepped inside. A beautiful young woman stood behind the counter watching him as he looked through the large assortment of cheap and expensive bottles of liquid fire. K-dawg kept his eyes peeled back for the person he was there to interrogate. He searched the empty isles and figured the man must have walked into the back room behind the register where someone stood post. He'd heard about the night of gambling here at the store once before but never thought to stop in and check it out. He approached the counter with a few bottles of liquor he didn't even plan to drink. He was being fueled by his thirst for retaliation, and he wanted nothing more than to make the intruders pay for his losses and the total disrespect.

"Will this be all?" the pretty woman asked, noting the huge roll of money K-dawg had purposely displayed.

"Could be," he replied without a hint of sexual intentions.

"Meaning?" she asked curiously.

"What's it gonna cost for admission," K-dawg cut to the chase, gesturing towards the back room and handing her the money for his liquor.

"Gambler—I should have figured that," she stated with a playful frown on her face.

"More than I drink," K-dawg smiled.

"Well, it's pretty expensive being that you're not a member." He could see the dollar signs flash in her light brown eyes as he decided to blow whatever he had to in order to get the info he needed from this guy.

"Name yo price."

***

K-dawg adjusted his eyes as he was escorted through the back door of the liquor store. Darkness enveloped the entire area as they walked one behind the other to the only door with light illuminating from underneath it. The burly guy before him stopped at the door and initiated a sequence of knocks before someone stepped to the door and looked through the slide at eye level. The men spoke for a quick second, then K-dawg was granted admission after several locks were removed and the steel door swung open. He greeted the doorman and was shown the way into the room where all the action was going on for the night.

"What you know, good, young blood?" Bossman greeted him as he welcomed him into his gambling establishment.

"Same ol' shit, old timer, just tryna get at some of them ol' hundids I know y'all got stashed away." K-dawg smiled, and Bossman laughed at the young savvy hustler before him.

"Fo' shit sho', youngin' they call me *The Bossman*, what's yo name?"

"K-dawg."

Hearing the name, most of the gamblers in the room recognized it and, or once upon a time, feared it. Some saluted him while others gave him a nod in welcoming, but the man he was there to see never turned around to greet him. Truth was, he spotted K-dawg outside the store but he never thought for a second that he would've made it into Bossman's spot. Bossman was always leery of the young crowd because of the drama that seemed to follow the young hustlas like a black cloud. But, now he was there and it was time to face his wrath.

K-dawg moved around the huge poker table, eyeing the players and acknowledging most. He kept a close eye on Pee Wee as he moved, and he could tell that the man was a nervous wreck from the perspiration that now showed above his smooth shaven upper lip. K-dawg continued to move around the table until he was towering over Pee Wee, still trying to figure out how he would punish the foolish hustler turned junkie.

"I think you're in my seat, hustla," K-dawg whispered into Pee Wee's ear. He could feel Pee Wee shivering once he patted his hand on the man's shoulder.

"My apologies, K-dawg, you know I ain't bringing no smoke nor do I want any," Pee Wee pleaded as he rose and stepped to the side.

"We'll see about that later, but for now I'll respect Boss' establishment and do a little gambling on you," K-dawg stated and took a seat while Pee Wee remained standing beside him.

"Is there a problem over there?" Bossman asked from across the room, and his doorman moved into view ready to pop off. K-dawg eyed the supposed security and immediately knew he'd take his ass if he approached him on some dumb shit.

Bossman watched as K-dawg punked Pee Wee for his seat at the table. Pee Wee was a long-time associate of Bossman's and he considered the guy a friend in many ways, and he didn't like what he'd just witnessed.

"Nawl, just letting the youngin' wet his feet, hell, I'm almost on flat anyway." Pee Wee backed down like a coward in order to save his true face. He didn't want K-dawg to get angry with him and possibly whoop his ass on the spot and expose him for the nasty habits he'd picked up.

"You familiar with the game, hustla?" asked the beautiful woman dealing the game.

"I learn quick," K-dawg flashed her a devilish grin. The woman smiled politely at his handsomeness and nodded before she began to do what she got paid so lovely to do.

K-dawg lifted the corners of his two cards and spotted the pair of pocket aces before lowering his hand and watching the other players around the table look at their hands in different manners. It had been a long since K-dawg even played a friendly game of poker, but he was an ESPN junkie and watched World Series Poker all the time, and knew that his pocket aces could win any hand in Texas Hold 'Em.

As the bets went around the table, he eyed the few hundred dollars in chips that Pee Wee had left. There were seven other players at the table and so far everyone had bet except for him. He once again eyed the small amount of chips left in front of him, then compared that with those of the other players chip count before making his decision.

"I'm all in," K-dawg said stone-faced.

"Whooa, youngsta, you know what you doin'?" Jack asked from the far side of the table.

"I've seen this on TV and it always worked for them, because the other players don't wanna call before seeing the cards flip over, and that wins me everyone's anti and gives me a little life over here." K-dawg laughed.

"Well, you won't be winning everybody's anti today, not with those pecans you betting with," one player stated and fell right into K-dawg's lure after matching the bet.

"Shit! I always gotta see the flop," the next gambler said and matched it as well as everyone else around the table.

K-dawg didn't give two shits if he won or lost, but he smiled at how well his con worked on the table. He really didn't expect for everyone to call him, but after seeing the pair of tens and an ace in the flop alone, he knew the pot would be his. He waited patiently as the other players made their side bets on the last two cards, but he knew he held the winning hand at the end and would be a few grand richer. That was if no one held pocket tens over him.

He was the first to expose his hand, and the layers at the table gasped and shook their heads at his boat-ace high. He swept up his winnings and requested a cash out right then and there. After getting quite a few sour faces and complaints, Bossman nodded to his worker and approved K-dawg's cash out.

"Youngsta, always keep yo' gambling good," Bossman stated and gestured towards the table as K-dawg counted out nearly five grand in free money.

K-dawg recognized the wisdom in Bossman's words and therefore handed each player one hundred and fifty bucks of their money back. Bossman stood and shook hands with K-dawg, then looked over the youngsta's shoulder and shook his head at Pee Wee.

"I need to holla at cha boy outside for a second if that's cool," K-dawg admitted after following Bossman's eyes.

"Shiit, the way I see it you're a paying customer and y'all business ain't none of mine," Bossman stated, then took his seat and stuffed his strong smelling cigar back in the corner of his lips.

"Pee Wee, outside!" K-dawg ordered and left the room. He stopped by the register to pick up the cheap liquor he paid for before entering the gambling spot.

"So, you're gonna leave with me disappointed in you," the beautiful woman spoke as he collected his purchase from her hand.

"Speak on it, ma."

"I'm Samantha, and you are?"

"I'm Kev, but everybody calls me K-dawg," he smiled flirtatiously.

"Okay, K-dawg, would it be cool if I asked you out on a date or would you have a crazy ass babymoma hunting us both down?" Sam chuckled at her own humor.

"Nawl, that's cool, ma, just DM me a time and date," K-dawg used his receipt and gave her his social media.

"Will do," Samantha replied sexily.

"Hope so," K-dawg said before walking out with Pee Wee close on his heels.

Once outside, K-dawg walked over to his car and put his back against the driver's side door and watched as Pee Wee nervously made his way over to him.

"Look, K-dawg, you know I'ma get you yo' bread. Actually, I'm—"

"Kill me with that shit, Wee. You owe me and my shit is due when I say it's due, big dawg, not the other way around. Now I came looking for you because I need information and I know you always keep a mean ass ear to the streets." K-dawg folded his massive arms across his chest and stared at the man before him.

"Somebody robbed my spot, killed a few of my soldiers, and I wanna know who was behind the hit, even if they didn't do it themselves no matter who they are," he made himself crystal clear so that Pee Wee wouldn't get confused on what he needed from him.

"I heard about some dudes getting robbed and killed but I had no idea that was your people. It won't be hard for me to get yesterday's news at all, plus ain't many niggas nutty enough to try yo' hand in these streets, so that narrows it down a lot!" Pee Wee stated, feeling a bit of relief since K-dawg wasn't there to beat him down or kill him for what he owed him.

"Find this out for me and you can consider all debts paid in full with me. I'll even start you over with a lil' somethin'," K-dawg promised.

"Say no more—I'm on it," Pee Wee agreed. "By the way, do you think I could um—Get my poker money back? I mean it's my only way to scratch back."

K-dawg reached inside of his pocket and came out with a big fuck you finger and laughed when Pee Wee started to reach for it before realizing he got got. It wasn't for just amusement though. The pathetic hustler turned junkie had owed K-dawg for two months and really didn't have intentions to clear that debt any time soon, and K-dawg knew that.

"Interest, Pee Wee, interest," K-dawg got in his whip and fired it up before peeling out, headed to find some helpful answers to his questions.

K-dawg was speeding through the many back streets in the hood to get to his spot, and niggas saluted as he passed. He had the hood's respect from his many years of putting in work as an enforcer for many of street legends both living and dead. It wasn't until Young Mack found him and put him on that he put his pistols and thirst for blood down. He had entered the game at such a young age that none of the hustlas growing up had any work for him. That was until he found out how easy it was to just pick up a gun and pop a nigga and not feel anything about it. He came up pretty quick once his young name hit the streets and his reputation built. He took to Young Mack quickly and fell in love with having a team by his side. Young Mack made it mandatory for him to have his own crew of hittas and hustlas to protect him as he got to the bag as one of Young Mack's head lieutenants. Shit was now taking a turn for the worse, and he was ready to put niggas in the dirt.

Riding through the hood with the top dropped felt relaxing but it did nothing to chill his boiling blood and the fire that was threatening to escape. He needed to talk to Young Mack before he flew off his handle. Just as he picked up his phone to call Young Mack for the hundredth time, his phone chimed, displaying an unfamiliar number.

"State the bidnezz," he answered as he pulled up to Wendy's drive-thru.

"Okay, I got a hit on some niggas moving a lot of work around your way. Could be the niggas that hit your spot but I cannot say for sure because I'm just not confident that these niggas are built for that type of drama, but they are slinging way more product than normal and that shit don't add up!"

Pee Wee stated as he undressed his brown bag special and got everything together to get high.

"So you expect me to just let niggas slide because you don't feel like they built for that life. Nigga, it's 2019, every nigga in the streets is built for that type of shit. Why you think niggas in these streets are dropping like flies outta the sky?" K-dawg couldn't believe Pee Wee had hit on more than he had in a matter of an hour compared to a whole day.

"One of my bitches put me on to 'em after I put a bug in her ear. She was already in the know about the situation with your spot, and my guess is these niggas been looking for some attention by boasting about the weight they moving."

"Wee, run me that homework and you let me worry about everything else. I don't give a fuck about guessing games. I only give a fuck about my dead soldiers, my missing coke and my missing money!" K-dawg stated before listening to everything Pee Wee had to give him.

"Bet! Keep yo ears to the earth and call me with anything you hear that sounds good enough to be used. I'm 'bout to paint the city red!" K-dawg said, then ended his call before trying Young Mack once again.

***

Young Mack groaned for the third time as his phone rang on the nightstand next to his bed. He saw the voicemails, missed calls and unread text messages and knew that he'd missed a busy morning. Sex with Ambrea wore him out like always, and the satisfied feeling he felt wouldn't allow him to apologize for all of the missed business opportunities on the other end of his phone.

He sat up and wiped sleep from his eyes just before the phone stopped ringing. Feeling unfazed by all the attention his line was getting, he made a mental note to get himself a back-up phone. It was still noon when he checked the time, so he really considered getting up now an early start for the day. He took a quick shower, brushed his teeth, then threw on a fresh pair of faded red Robin jeans. He matched them with a red long-sleeve Versace top, and slipped on a fresh pair of white Nike *Air Force 1's* with the red check and red bottom.

His phone went off again as he stepped outside and faced the unbalanced Texas weather. The morning had left behind a nice cold drift that had not been there last night which reached the height of eighty-nine degrees. He dropped his head after hearing the familiar ringtone. "Damn, I forgot about him," he said to himself before answering.

"What's good, my guy?" Young Mack answered as he walked to his ride.

"Jack boys! Nigga, I been blowing this damn line up!" K-dawg yelled hysterically into his end of the phone.

"Whooa, back up, what did you say!"

"J.a.c.k.b.o.y.s, nigga, is that clear enough for you! Somebody hit our shit and I'm 'bout to paint this city red until I find the mu'fuckas that was brazy enough to do this shit."

Young Mack could feel the heat radiating from the other end of their call and knew his guy was burning up inside. "Damn, that's twice," Young Mack said mostly to himself.

"Don't make a move without me, homey, I'm on my way!" Young Mack said to K-dawg.

"I ain't making no promises, so yo ass better hurry up and get here," K-dawg said, ending their call. Young Mack hurried to make another call as he started his whip.

"Talk to me," Chris answered even though he was gambling. Young Mack could hear the bets being called in the background.

"I need to speak with Hog," Young Mack called out over his speakerphone. He heard movements and voices rising shortly before his guy was on the line.

"Hog here, what's poppin', big bruh?"

"Time to get dirty, mufucka, meet me at the spot!"

"Say less," Hog stated, then ended their call.

Young Mack wasn't surprised to see Deuce standing outside of the doorway waiting for him to arrive. He hadn't called Deuce but the fact that Deuce and K-dawg were the best of friends in junior high and now shared a closeness that blood brothers would envy, he knew K-dawg had called him.

"Everything's ready," Deuce said once Young Mack approached him on the porch.

"What about Hog? He here yet?" Young Mack asked, looking around.

"All here, gangsta," Hog responded once he heard Young Mack's voice outside.

"Let's get to it then."

Deuce watched as a normally cool and relaxed Young Mack drove through the back streets. His jawline flexed from the way he tightened his face into a scowl, and Deuce smiled at the old saying passed around through the grape vines.

"The quietest one in the room is usually the deadliest," he spoke the words out loud. Young Mack caught the reference but he was in his own zone and wasn't gonna let nothing knock that, not even the words of his father. Five minutes later they were hopping outta Young Mack's ride and approaching the front door of the trap house K-dawg operated out of.

K-dawg opened the door after hearing the right knocks in the right succession. Young Mack stepped in, followed by Deuce and Hog who all stared hard at the beautiful females on their hands and knees doing their best to scrub the crimson colored stains out of the carpet in the living room. The room was still heavily disarrayed, and they could only imagine how the other rooms must have looked.

"What do we know?" Young Mack cut to the chase and got to business.

"Shit, all I know is some niggas came around asking about you, some niggas I ain't never seen you with before. I shot them bitches my best finger and grabbed my nuts on 'em!" K-dawg fumed.

"No shit, niggas did come looking for you at the spot too," Deuce remembered.

"Did y'all get names?" Young Mack asked, puzzled.

"Nawl, I didn't give a fuck to. Niggas come around looking for my nigga and I don't know 'em, fuck 'em all day long!" K-dawg flexed.

"Fuck! We gotta find out who did this shit and make 'em pay for it!" Young Mack spoke with fire in his heart. He was about to speak again but his phone chimed, and he knew the call was important and he couldn't miss it.

"What's the word, beautiful?" he answered after the second ring.

"That's the second time today that someone called me that. I definitely must be doing something, right!" Ambrea smiled because she liked to tease him and make him a bit jealous. Her mood changed quickly once she realized he wasn't gonna respond.

"Hello?" she said, hoping he hadn't hung up on her.

"Yeah, I'm here, ma, but I'm in the middle of some important shit right now," he explained, not wanting to deal with her gleeful bantering.

"And from the sound of your voice it must be bad," she paused before continuing. "I checked into that Kanye situation out west like you suggested, and I hate to bring you even more tension, but things are already being put on hold." Young Mack dropped his shoulders after hearing that.

"I'm sorry, babe, do you need me to be there when you make it in?" Ambrea loved being in his presence.

"That'll be nice, ma, just let me wrap things up out here and I'll be there."

"I love you," Ambrea admitted for the first time since their romance had begun.

"One hunid, baby girl," Young Mack ended their call. He wasn't sure how to respond to her words at the moment but he knew they would have to have a talk once he made it in from taking care of his street business.

"What was that?" Deuce asked after watching his reaction to whoever was on the other end of that conversation.

"Trust me, kid, at a time like this you don't even wanna know what that was about," Young Mack warned him. Deuce was never the type to apply pressure to situations that didn't warrant it, so he took Young Mack's word for it and backed off.

"So all we know about this is that some niggas rode through looking for me and we don't know who because no one asked—"

"It was two cats—I know that much," Deuce interjected.

"I counted two heads myself," K-dawg agreed.

Everything they were telling him was registering in his head but the boiling anger he felt after being burned yet again would not allow for him to think straight. This was the second time, and he wasn't letting the streets slide by with this one. His father couldn't say anything to stop him from making the streets bleed this time.

"What did we lose?" Young Mack asked, needing to hear it from K-dawg's mouth.

"Three soldiers, a queen and our whole stash."

"Two niggas wouldn't have been able to just walk in here and do all this damage and leave yo big ass unscratched. What the fuck are we dealing with here?" Young Mack asked furiously.

"Unscratched my ass! Nigga knocked me the fuck out!" K-dawg said through clenched teeth. He turned around so they could get a good look at the gruesome wound his shorty had stitched up for him the entire time he was trying to get Young Mack on the line.

"Caught me out back taking out more work," K-dawg confessed.

"Damn," Deuce said as he examined the swollen flesh behind K-dawg's head.

"That's not a two-man job," Young Mack concluded.

"I never said that it was. All I know is them niggas came through here looking for you and an hour later our shit is being ravished by god-knows-who," K-dawg stated.

"Fuck it! We'll turn this bitch out until we know who did it, then dead they asses too, all of 'em!" Young Mack decided it was time to make mu'fuckas answer for stepping on his toes. He wasn't willing to take any other setbacks without heavy retaliation.

"That's what the fuck I'm talkin' 'bout," Hog smiled before pulling back the zipper on the bag Deuce had carried inside with them.

"Let's do that!" Deuce growled, getting pumped and ready to make a statement and show the streets that they were not the mu'fuckas to try.

Chapter Six

"Rolla, bitch, what's poppin'?" K-dawg saluted as he and one of his little homeys greeted each other.

"You know me, what's up with it?" Rolla asked as he locked hands with K-dawg.

"Tryna stay sucka free in a land full of lollipops, you know how this shit goes. Check game though, blood, you strapped?" K-dawg asked, masking his frustration.

"Like a baby in a car seat, nigga, you know what it is!" he replied, showing his work.

"You know I love ya like a lil' brotha, right?" K-dawg said, locking hands with him once again.

"Who we finna fuck up—I know you and I'ma ride regardless so fuck with me," Rolla said, getting hyped.

"Every nigga in this house is 'bout to be dog food. You see that van over there."

Rolla turned his head and quickly spotted the blacked out van posted at the end of the block. Instinctively, his hand immediately reached for his heat, stopping only after feeling K-dawg's hand restricting his.

"I'm on my ass for even coming out here to warn you, but I know you would much rather rock with me than to protect these pussies."

"Damn, you 'bout to make me not like you!" Rolla said as he stared in K-dawg's eyes.

"This ain't what you want, lil' bruh, I'm out here tryna save yo ass, so look—you can either rock with me and my team or get rocked to sleep along with these niggas because they dying for sure tonight!" K-dawg warned as he released his grip on Rolla's wrist.

"Who's in the van?" Rolla asked, tryna assess the situation.

"Not important," Young Mack spoke as he stepped out from behind Rolla.

"Man, what the fuck!" Rolla damn near jumped outta his own skin.

"Keep yo voice down," Young Mack stated and waved his arm above his head once. Deuce and Hog slid casually out of the van, carrying their weapons at their sides.

"You have a choice to make," Young Mack said, staring at Rolla. "You can either walk us through the front door or you can catch pussy and go wait to drive the van when we come out."

"Pussy? Nigga, I created the name *dickhead*, my gee, you better let them in on my get down," Rolla spoke, holding his nuts the way Young Mack always remembered K-dawg doing when making a point.

"What's funny?" Deuce asked a smiling K-dawg.

"Official!" K-dawg responded shortly. He didn't want to let them in on how Rolla rocked; he wanted them to see it for themselves.

Rolla listened to everything that Young Mack and K-dawg told him they needed him to do. It was nothing compared to the smallest he'd ever done, so he was down for the play. As grimy as shit may have seemed to the others, what they didn't know was the reason behind Rolla sitting outside and not on the inside like he'd normally be.

Rolla took his time creeping back inside the house, not bothering to lock the door behind him. Hearing the music blasting from the back, he knew his supposed crew was still back there giving their attention to the fine yellow-boned chick doing her best to entertain them. He stopped in the hall and checked his Ruger for the safety, clicking it off. He then moved until he stood in the door frame of the den and watched as the sexy ass broad filled her mouth with the dick that was popping up between her big tits. She was moaning like crazy as Mark pounded her from the back. Rolla did a quick scan of the room and noticed that Webster wasn't there. Webster was the hardest outta these guys and he would really have to seek him out before dealing with these clowns. His jaw tightened as he stood there seething; his handle broke as he watched the yellow broad control the dick in her hand as it sprayed come all over her face and tits.

He texted K-dawg and told him to keep the others outta his way as he did his best shit on the inside. He promised to leave a scene straight out of a horror film for them to inspect after he was finished. K-dawg quickly replied with a 'go ahead' emoji, and Rolla set out to do just that.

"How we know he gone work with us over them if we out here and he in there with them?" Deuce protested but K-dawg shot that shit down. He knew Rolla all too well and he understood that nothing was really safe around that young dude.

"How 'bout you go check the scene out once he's finished," K-dawg stated, and Deuce accepted his challenge. K-dawg always thought Rolla had some loose screws growing up in the streets. That was until he saw Rolla's work firsthand and he realized the kid didn't have screws in his head at all; dude was sick for real, and K-dawg admired that about him.

Rolla stepped away from the doorway in search of Webster. He quickly made his way into the kitchen and grabbed a big-handled cutting knife. He then put his Ruger in the waistline of his True Religion jeans and tucked the knife into his back pocket. The living room was clear, so Rolla crept from bedroom to bedroom and still found nothing. Deciding to just get shit poppin', he reached for his Ruger as he made his way back towards the den but was stopped short after hearing the faint sound of sex escaping from behind a cracked hallway-closet door. He quickly moved his hand away from his burner and gripped the knife in his back pocket. He listened carefully at the door. Sure enough, the sound of someone having sex was coming from behind that door, exposing Webster doing the unthinkable.

"Ro—Rolla, damn, what you busting up in here on a nigga like that for!" Webster bellowed out from his low position on the closet's floor.

"The fuck you doin'!" Rolla asked with his face twisted up.

"Shiit, I was just tryna holla at my babymoma without all that loud ass music." Webster lied. He was desperately trying to hide the fact that he was lying inside that closet beating his dick while they had live pussy in the other room. "What's with the knife?" he asked, changing the subject, but thought it weird for him to be holding it.

"About to chop up some work, but fuck all that, get yo ass outta this closet." Rolla pretended to put the knife into his back pocket as he took a slight step backwards to give Webster some room. He watched closely as Webster began to get up with his back turned towards the door in an effort to hide himself while he put his shit back into his pants. That move proved to be the worst move he could have ever made and it cost him his life as Rolla smoothly stepped behind him and pressed the ultra-sharp blade through the back of Webster's neck. Webster gargled and spit out globs of blood before Rolla lowered his body to the closet floor and noticed as his cell phone dropped from his grip. Rolla bent down and scooped it up to make sure that he wasn't video chatting at the time of his murder, but what he saw made him cringe. He would have never guessed Webster to be gay but the shit playing on his phone was more than enough and explained why he was missing out on all the action the others were enjoying in the other room.

Rolla left Webster's dead body and phone and made his way to the back of the house once again. The show was still going strong once he reached the doorway. Both niggas were fucking the shit outta the thick ass yellow-bone; they were giving it to her double penetration style and she was loving every minute of it. She was sitting cowgirl on one dick while the other drilled her up the ass. It was a perfect setting in Rolla's eyes as he pulled out his Ruger .9mm but held the knife tight in his other hand. He approached them from behind with ease while aiming the lethal blade between Joe's ass cheeks.

With one strong lunge Rolla had the blade shoved in to the handle up his anal cavity. The pain was so chilling that Joe couldn't find his voice to scream out while releasing his bowels and bladder simultaneously.

"Oh—shit, nigga, cum in this phat ass," the yellow-bone said, thrilled.

"Damn, nigga you getting that nasty shit on my legs!" Mark complained but kept right on thrusting up into her wet pussy.

"Hold the fuck up! Bitch, is you pissing in me?" She screamed in horror after seeing Joe's eyes rolled to the back of his head.

He was indeed pissing inside of her and his bowels were escaping nonstop while blood rained from around the knife stuffed up his ass. The room reeked of sex and shit, and nearly caused Rolla to puke his guts out.

Rolla had seen enough. He kicked Joe hard in his back causing him to fall forward, dropping his dead weight on top of the other two. The chick was screaming her head off of her back. Her screams ceased and her eyes nearly popped outta her head once she saw Rolla who was using her shirt to wipe his hands clean.

"Bitch, get up!" Mark yelled from the bottom of the three, but she couldn't move. Fear had her frozen in place.

She instantly regretted ever taking these niggas up on their offer to pay her to dance for them. Because without her knowledge or consent, someone had slipped mollies in her liquor and got her lit. She took the pills pretty often, so it didn't take long to figure out that someone had given them to her. Now she regretted everything about her favorite pills, and the fact that Rolla had caught her red handed had sealed her fate; his loyalty to K-dawg had sealed that of the others.

Rolla walked over and used the shirt he had been wiping his hands with to pull the knife from Joe's ass. He tripped on how smoothly the blade went in, but took even more strength to force it outta there. He stared into the woman's eyes; the eyes were pleading with him to have mercy on her, but he wasn't for it. She had done the ultimate betrayal and he could never forgive her or get over that. She knew her time on earth was coming to a close, and she too released her bladder.

Rolla somehow took sympathy on the slimy cheating bitch; maybe it was outta love, he wasn't sure where the shit was coming from, but he just couldn't let her make it outta there alive. He aimed his Ruger and put one between her eyes and rocked her to sleep. Mark grew hysterical after hearing the roar of his gun going off.

"Man, whoever you are, dawg, I got bread and I got work, please just let me live!" he cried out but his pleas fell on deaf ears.

Rolla knew that Mark was one of those thug imposters, but he actually liked him, more than just using him for his dope and trap time.

"You saying that while lying here with your dick buried in my bitch," Rolla stated. "My ex-bitch that is!" He laughed.

"Rolla! Blood, she came over here wildin', kid, you know how she was!" Mark tried defending his own actions by putting Rolla's dead chick at blame.

"First off, nigga, yo ain't BLOOD, so you definitely dying for saying that," Rolla said, and put one through Mark's opened mouth.

"Secondly, you's one disloyal ass, bitch nigga," Rolla used all of his might to move the first two bodies from on top of Mark before taking his time to carve up his body real nice. Once he finished, he put one in Joe's head then turned on his heels and never looked back.

K-dawg smiled when he saw Rolla walking outta the house. Deuce wasn't going to back down on his words, so he made his way past Rolla, headed straight for the front door of the trap house Rolla just left out of.

"Be careful, homey!" K-dawg laughed as Deuce entered the house. Rolla remained silent and removed from the others while Deuce ran off to do whatever it was he planned to do.

"I told you!" K-dawg balled over in laughter as Deuce shot up outta there like his ass was on fire. Young Mack and Hog couldn't hold back either after seeing Deuce be all animated.

"You one sick lil' mu'fucka, mu'fucka!" Deuce said, holding tight to his stomach.

"That's my dawg, that's my dawg!" K-dawg laughed as he mimicked the words to a jam he'd heard earlier on the radio.

"I take it that you're driving?" Young Mack laughed.

"Fuck no, my shit hurts, let Hog drive," Deuce said with a queasy look on his face.

"I'll drive but it looks like you should walk," Hog joked and patted Deuce on the back.

"Fuck y'all! It's one thing to pop a nigga, but it's another to carve a nigga up like he did ol' boy in there."

"Loyalty over everything," Rolla finally broke his silence.

"Mufucka, I can read!" Deuce said, then hopped inside the van as everyone laughed around him.

"Official," K-dawg announced before they filed inside of the van one by one.

***

"Doe! Bet back—Doe! Try both ways on this ten and four, anybody else thank sum'n fake about that clock in London?" Malli boasted as he shook up the dice.

"I got half a quarter, you crap, nigga!"

"I see why they call you Grams now, nigga. I thought it was because you liked stuntin' on Instagram, but half a quill, kid, that's kinda low even for you, big dog." Malli shook his head.

"I think you thinking about the wrong kind of quarter, lil' fish in the big pond," Grams capped back. He then reached inside of his jacket pocket and pulled out four and a half ounces of coke. Malli's eyes lit up once he saw the dollar signs attached to winning what Grams held in his hand. The dice were in his favor tonight. As much as he paid for them, they had better be, or Arab Tariq would've been meeting his maker.

"Bet that, homey," Malli agreed.

"Nawl, match that before you stroke them dice, my dude," Grams replied.

"Oh yeah, where's my manners!" Malli joked as he dropped blue Franklins all over the drugs Grams had put up.

"Come on and shoot, playful ass nigga!" Rick butted in, ready for the big outcome.

"Yeah, Malli, yo letting these ducks wet their tails while you slowin' up that money roll," Kool said. Kool was Malli's little brother through the slums they grew up in together. Nothing in life could separate the two of them, and they shared everything. Mostly weed, money and pussy.

"I'm 'bout to knock does down with my first shot, lil' bruh, just chill and be very still," Malli shook the dice before schoolin' 'em one at a time.

"Coming out big ass clocks!" Malli damn near shit himself when he looked up and saw the five masked men surrounding them on the basketball court.

"Shoot, nigga, ain't no getting off that!" Grams said, rubbing his hands together.

Boom!

"Oh shit!" Grams screamed behind the thunderous sound of the cannon knocking Malli's noodles loose.

"Don't nut up now, toughy! You said shoot, right?" K-dawg mocked Grams. Young Mack stepped forward and watched the group of hustlas closely before speaking.

"Who hit my spot on Canfield and Dennis? Someone delivered capital punishment to my soldiers for getting money on their own blocks and I wanna know who did it," Young Mack circled the rest of them as he talked and watched their reactions.

"Man, this the Bricks, poppa, we don't know shit about that!" Kool spoke up after no one else would.

"So that's y'all's statement?" Young Mack stopped in his tracks, then faced the men on the ground.

After a moment of silence, Deuce didn't need to see a sign, the light was already green. He let his choppa (AK-47) rip, nearly decapitating his first target while Hog followed through with a couple of thunderous claps from his automatic pump.

Chapter Seven

"Shit gone be hot in the streets for a while," Young Mack said as he looked out over the city's skyline.

He and K-dawg had sat for hours thinking over their current situation and discussing ways for their operation to continue to see a profit no matter what came their way. The streets needed supplying, and someone had to be there to supply them, and K-dawg figured that someone needed to be them, war or not.

"So what's next?" K-dawg asked, needing to know their direction.

"I'm not even sure," Young Mack sighed as he turned to face his top lieutenant.

"Damn," K-dawg couldn't believe what he'd just heard. Young Mack was never the one to be at a loss of words. Life was like one big ass chess game for Young Mack, and he respected and followed him religiously.

"Think we need to relocate the spot?" K-dawg asked after a long silence.

"I think mu'fuckas oughta get the picture now," Young Mack replied without thinking it through.

"Fo shit sho they will," K-dawg respected his decision and was willing to ride no matter what they chose to do.

"A'ight, I see that you're not gonna tell me what's goin' on without me asking, so I'ma ask," K-dawg spoke up. "What did you mean by you'd been hit twice, because niggas bled and ceased breathing for fuckin' with the home team, and why wasn't I aware of any time other than this one?" He sat back and opened the floor for Young Mack to explain everything that was going on around them.

"As much as I love and respect you, lil' bruh, I never mix my hustles, so there is nothing for me to explain to you about that. Tell you what though, I want you to go ahead and relocate the trap and head shit from a different location. One that we already have established though, nothing new just yet. We need a few niggas with work playing the corner of the old spot to redirect our walk-in clientele. Make sure we keep a shooter with them while they're out there too!" Young Mack ordered.

"Good idea and I respect your mind, your decisions, and your gangsta, bleed. Just know that if you need me for any reason, and I mean any reason," K-dawg lifted his new Draco pistol, "I'm there!"

"Overstood!" Young Mack laughed and embraced his soldier before he split.

Young Mack moved back to the huge bay windows that overlooked the city from his condo's view. He was seriously contemplating what his next move would be. Niggas had violated, blood had been shed, yet his mind still wasn't at ease. He made a mental note to visit his pops and utilize his keen knowledge of masterminding the game.

He poured himself a stiff shot of Hennessy while deep in thought. He didn't drink much but the times he did they certainly called for it, and now was one of those times. He moved into his bedroom and walked into his closet before moving a few things around until he came face to face with a dummy wall he'd set up to hide his safe. He played with the wall until he exposed his stainless steel safe. It wasn't the only one he owned but he used it to stash the things he'd frequently need.

After entering the code and using his thumbprint, he opened the safe and emptied its contents. Once he had everything out, he began his count. He was closing in on three hundred grand, and still had twelve perfectly wrapped and compressed bricks of cocaine left. He hated the loses he and his teams had taken over the past months, but his father always taught him to accept the game as it comes. Didn't mean he had to like it, though. He'd just hit K-dawg off with two bricks for operation, enough to get him back into position once he was done with that. He would have to do the same with Deuce and the others which would leave him at eight bricks to last them for only God-knows-how-long.

He put the money and the leftover eight bricks back into his safe. The other four bricks he placed inside different shoe boxes still inside of their retail store bags, then placed them along the wall by his bedroom door.

"Everything okay?" Ambrea's voice startled him a bit. She was standing in the doorway of the bedroom when he turned around and saw her there looking jazzy as ever.

Her hair was pulled back into a long slick ponytail, and the baby hair along her forehead made him picture the famous singer, Mya. Ambrea was beautiful in all ways, and he loved that about her along with the way she rode for him like no other he'd ever been with. Her curves were covered in one of the many catsuits she loved fitting herself into. This one was white with ruffled material that exposed her naked flesh beneath. His mouth watered at the sight of her flawless toes peeping through her Zanotti sandals.

"For now," he said, moving into her space.

"Don't panic, baby, things will pick up again, they always do. Plus he knows you are solid and he's never had any problems with your end before, so I'm sure it'll be okay!" she said before pressing her soft lips onto his. Their tongues found each other as they held onto one another.

Young Mack was definitely stressed out and knew that something needed to shake or he'd be pulling jobs sooner than his father imagined he would. He was almost at his quitting point, but things kept getting more and more bizarre without warning.

"I know it will, shit just ain't to my liking right now. I got the shit with pop's lawyer hanging in the balance and everything is riding on me. Not just with pops but with my whole crew. They relying on me to lead the way and keep us together so that everybody can eat and now yo ol' man is pumping the brakes on our normal shipments, shit just crazy all over the place." Ambrea could see the weight and pressure he was feeling when he talked. She wished dearly that she could be the one to lift that weight from his shoulders but everything he was going through was out of her reach. There was nothing she could do to solve his problem until things cooled off at the borders.

She sat down next to him on the foot of his bed and put her arm around his shoulder and for the very first time she noticed the huge painted mural of a beautiful woman draped in diamonds. The woman looked like royalty.

"Who's that," Ambrea asked.

"Huh?" Young Mack raised his head from the palms of his hands and looked at her. He followed her eyes and saw that she was looking at the image he'd had painted fresh from his memory. The artist did one helluva job and Young Mack loved the work and promised to hire him in the future.

"She's a queen," he replied and stood from the bed. He walked past her view of the painting and stepped inside of his closet to change clothes.

"Which queen is she and from where?" Ambrea asked, even more curious to know what his infatuation with this woman was.

"One that no other in life could ever compare to," he spoke from his heart.

"She's beautiful, the artist did a great job," she stated, admiring the portrait.

"Yeah, she truly is, inside and out."

"You know her personally?" she asked, stepping into the closet behind him.

"I can't find nothing in here, let's go shopping." He tried changing the subject but she wasn't having it.

"Who is that woman in the painting, Mackentosh Miller the second?" She drilled him as they headed for the door.

"Grab those bags, we'll talk in the car," he promised as he removed items from a pair of jeans and put everything into the pockets of his Gucci pajamas.

***

Rob was really feeling the burn of not being able to pull jobs. Young Mack was nowhere to be found, and he hadn't as much as heard from him since they were robbed. He was really hurting financially and couldn't stand to go another week or even a day without plotting to put some bands in his pocket.

"You sure about this?" Max asked him as they neared the sports bar a close associate had directed Rob to if he were looking for his kind of work.

Rob wasn't used to anything other than taking something for a living. He'd never worked a nine-to-five in his young life, and wasn't ever going out like that in this white America. Drugs weren't his thing either because he knew nothing about selling them.

"How yo pockets lookin', nigga?" Rob asked Max with a deep scowl on his face.

"Shit, I'm so broke my pockets hate my pants, my nigga!" Max capped.

"So stop asking me stupid shit, let's go," Rob stated and parked his ride. He climbed out and wasn't waiting for Max to catch his heels.

The sports bar was lit once they got inside and made it to the bar. Max took in their surroundings and smiled as bad ass women passed, giving them the eye. Rob was on some different shit as he too observed the crowded place. He was looking for anyone that fit the description of the guy he was given, the guy who would help him find jobs of his caliber.

Half an hour had passed, and Rob felt that there was something other than sports keeping the place this crowded so early in the evening. But he was on a mission and he wasn't feeling the *Finding Waldo* shit anymore. He moved back to the bar where he spotted a super sexy bartender working hard to keep orders filled and drinks flowing.

"Can I help you?" the sexy bartender asked after she noticed him watching her heavy.

"That depends on how much weight you hold around here," Rob cut straight to the chase. He was tired of playing games and waiting on someone to show up that obviously wasn't gonna show.

"Speak on it," she replied, giving him her undivided attention. He liked how sexy she looked standing there with her arms folded across her chest.

"I'm looking for Bunny but since the nigga obviously ain't showing up, fuck it, I need to see the big man," Rob explained.

"And by *big man* you mean, who, Phatts?" she asked with raised eyebrows.

"Yeah, he here," Rob sat back on the stool, prepared to wait as long as he had to in order to speak with someone that could put some money in his pockets. Before going into action, she observed him for a few seconds and realized that he was serious.

"Let me check," she replied and turned to pick up the cordless phone behind the bar. She remained quiet as someone split on the other end of the phone while she looked him over.

She removed the phone from her ear and placed it under the bar, "Men's restroom, middle stall, flush three times quickly," she ordered before handing him a straight shot of vodka. He looked like he could use the drink, plus he was about to see Phatts, and he'd need his nerves to be in check.

Rob downed the strong drink then thanked her. He ordered Max to stay there until he returned. Max readily agreed, not wanting to leave all the asses he'd been watching walk by. Max watched as Rob entered the restroom, followed by two burly looking men. The bartender warned him not to join in on that and he quickly sat back in his seat.

Rob wasn't expecting for anyone to be following him, but he quickly found himself being jammed between the two men that came in behind him and the wall.

"Assume the position, youngin'," one of the guys said and Rob complied.

"He's clear."

"Middle stall like she told you," the second guy's deep voice spoke before they left the restroom.

He entered the stall and did as he was told. After three quick flushes, he watched as the entire wall including the toilet slid back then turned half circle, exposing the hidden office tucked behind the wall.

Phatts eyed the young man as he nervously stepped into his office. He remembered the face immediately, and so did Skooby who instinctively reached for his pistol. Phatts shook his head softly, putting Skooby on ice; he already knew what he was thinking. Phatts knew the young hustla couldn't be stupid enough to try their hand, plus he was unarmed and looked a bit nervous. Phatts sat back in his custom leather desk chair and interlocked his fingers.

"Who are you and what the hell you doing in my establishment looking for me?" Phatts spoke firmly.

"No disrespect intended, but I'm Rob and I was guided here through one of your employees, but dude must've lost his way."

"So why didn't you lose yours?" Skooby mumbled.

"Do I answer him?" Rob asked, amused by dude's interjection. He kept his eyes on Phatts without looking in the other guy's direction.

"Why would you ask me that?" Phatts was intrigued by the balls on the youngsta.

"Because he's not over there," Rob pointed to where Phatts sat behind the big oakwood desk.

"Lil' nigga, I'll blow yo mufuckin' head off yo shoulders," Skooby jumped to his feet with his weapon in hand.

"Skooby, chill the hell out, he's just a kid!" Phatts ordered, and he did as he was told.

"I'm far from a kid, but coming from a legend like yourself I'll definitely accept that," Rob stated, being honest.

He had a lot of respect for the name, Phatts, and to actually be in his presence and speaking with him had his mind on a whole different level.

"I'm well aware of you being here, young man, but Bunny didn't lose his way, he lost his credibility," Phatts stood from behind his desk.

Rob knew exactly what Phatts was implying and hoped that didn't apply to him being there too. He silently thought about the dumb shit Bunny must've done to get himself rocked to sleep. Rob put his hands behind his back as Phatts approached him.

"Now, what's your request from ol' Phatts?"

"Me and my guys need work. No drugs and definitely no murders," Rob looked over at Skooby, then back to Phatts before continuing.

"We break into shit, rob shit on any level, and even do a little kidnapping if need be, but that's about as far as our talents take us," Rob explained.

Phatts liked the fact that he made everything clear to him. He was already aware of the things the youngsta and his crew did. Hell, the fact that he was standing there looking for work after playing victim to Phatts and his crew was humorous as hell to Phatts, but he chose to remain professional about the situation.

Phatts moved back behind his desk and took a seat. He pulled out a leather case and removed a thick cigar and placed it under his nose. After inhaling the strong fragrance coming from the foreign leaf, he clipped the tail end then placed it in his mouth while rotating it, the whole time never losing eye contact with Rob.

He's a helluva hustla, Phatts thought to himself as he put fire to the tip of his cigar. Clouds of smoke rose above and danced around his smooth bald head as he let out cloud after cloud from his mouth before pointing at Rob.

"I got a lil' somethin' lined up for you. Come to think about it, it'll give my guys a break to enjoy their families for a while," Phatts reached into his desk and came out with what they called the homework. *Homework* was details on a certain gig, and he was entrusting Rob on this one. Phatts knew that he worked alongside Young Mack and knew that if he gave them the job, things would pan out just the way he needed them to.

"I got this," Rob stated. He was familiar with the projected establishment.

"The take on this one will be sixty-forty my way, take it or leave it!" Phatts stated.

"Take!" Rob replied while backing out of the office before anything could change Phatts' mind.

Phatts smiled as the wall to his office closed and Rob was gone. Having Young Mack and his crew operating under his thumb would prove to be millions-of-dollars-worthy.

"You think he'll produce?" Skooby asked while surfing his social media page.

"Of course they will," Phatts reclined.

He instantly sat back up at the sound of his wife calling his emergency line. Seeing her face brought about a different smile to his than what his face held earlier.

"Hey, my love, what's on your mind?" he answered, unprepared for what news that was about to be delivered.

Skooby could sense that there was a problem when silence overtook Phatts' phone call. He looked up to see the tight scowl on his face and thought about the bodies that were about to drop.

"Everything good?" Skooby asked once he was off the phone.

"Somebody shot my son, he's in ICU fighting for his life as we speak," Phatts confessed.

"What are we waiting for?" Skooby jumped up and went into the closet and brought out two H&K MP5 assault rifles.

"Load 'em up, but first we gotta get to that hospital, my wife's there waiting." Phatts rose and nearly lost his balance before grabbing ahold of his desk.

"You good?" Skooby asked, rushing to his aid.

"Yeah, I'm straight, let's go."

Chapter Eight

"Let's just go to Young Mack," Ash suggested as Rob tried even harder to get him to join them on a job.

"Go ahead and call him, and if he answers then we go to him and if he doesn't then you rock with us." Rob gambled as he watched Ash mentally deliberate with himself.

Ashton hadn't been completely honest with Rob lately. He had heard from Young Mack almost every day since their loss, but what he wasn't sure of was why Young Mack wasn't answering or staying in contact with Rob.

"Okay, I'll hit him up and see what he can come up with," Ash decided as he stood to leave the room for privacy.

"Nawl, kid, hit dude now, we need you because the lick is set for tonight at closing time," Rob pressured him.

Ash sighed heavily from the pressure Rob was applying to him. He wasn't trying to let Rob and Max down or turn down a chance at getting some quick cash, but he needed Young Mack's blessing. They were a team; no matter how fucked up things might have been between them, he wasn't trying to go against what they built. Young Mack was his guy, and Rob was too; he'd go to back for either one of them, and right now Rob was really bringing it.

Fuck it, Ash thought to himself as he pulled out his phone and dialed Young Mack's number.

"You know who you reached," Young Mack's voicemail stated over Ash's speaker phone.

Rob smiled and requested him to try again outta good faith.

"You know who you reached," the automated voice record repeated same as the first time.

"Just like I thought, you rockin', right?" Rob asked, throwing his arm around Ash's shoulder. He wasn't really trying to put him under any kind of pressure, but he needed him behind the wheel for this job.

"Yeah, guess I am," Ash said while calling Young Mack once again, hoping that he was alright. He had never missed Ash's call more than once, and something just didn't feel right.

The phone rang a few times but no one answered, so he gave up and gave Rob his undivided attention. Rob was lit as he explained the sweet lick to Ash and Max. They were tucked away inside the basement of Rob's house, smoking kush and playing PlayStation 5, waiting for the right time to take it to the streets.

"This shit really is like taking candy from a baby," Rob said, excited, after reviewing the homework for the job they were about to pull off.

"Young Mack always said that place is hazardous," Ash pointed out. He was dead focused on the ass whooping he was putting on Max in NFL Madden.

"Young Mack ain't here, nigga! That nigga gives two fucks if we eat or starve. How many times you hear from him since we took that loss, huh?" Rob was heated.

"Doesn't matter, poppa, loyalty is everything." Ash shot him a stale face.

"No caps, I'm with the whole loyalty get up, but Ash, I'm hungry out here and I ain't turning my back on a chance to eat."

"I hear you," Ash said, giving his attention back to the video game.

Rob stepped in front of the television and stared both guys in their eyes. He couldn't for the life of him understand how they were getting ready to pull off a dangerous job and his men couldn't pull their heads out of the video world. He needed Ash to be on this job with them in a major way. Ash was like the guy in the *Transporter* movies behind the wheel, and they needed his skills pretty badly.

"Ash, I'm asking you as a friend and as someone who understands how much loyalty means to you. Are you rockin' with us on this thing or what, because I need you!" Rob confessed.

The whole situation with Rob and doing the job was about to drive Ashton crazy. He sat back on the sofa and really analyzed the severity of this job and just how desperate Rob was to get some bands in his pockets. Hell, he too needed some cash and knew that they could pull this job off after reviewing the homework, but he wasn't tryna defy Young Mack's orders for them to fall back for a while.

***

"So the pretty lady in the painting is your mother?" Ambrea was shocked after hearing that.

"Yeah, that's her," Young Mack replied with pride. Young Mack loved both of his parents more than he loved his own life, and he could see the admiration in Ambrea's eyes as he talked.

"Where is she?" Ambrea asked as he watched his cell ring for like the hundredth time since they came out shopping.

He knew it was her brother calling but with his hands full of shopping bags and the dangerous potential of him finding out about them, he realized that he just couldn't answer, not yet.

"Uhh—She's around," Young Mack stated, uninterested in talking about his mother and her situation. Thinking about her made him miss her more than he already did and due to certain reasons he wasn't prepared to visit her, but the want never died away.

He dropped the thoughts of his mother immediately after he thought he saw someone he knew. Ambrea followed him as he maneuvered through shoppers to get a good view.

As he closed the distance between them, he took in everything about the woman they were now close to. He'd had his eyes on her as they moved, and from that distance there wasn't a doubt in his mind, and now that he was closer he just really wasn't sure. He hadn't seen or heard from her in a lifetime but his gut was telling him he was right, so he decided to make himself seen.

"Young Mack, how you, my dude!" a young male waiter spoke as Young Mack approached the register at the Starbucks he frequented pretty often.

"I'm coolin', how 'bout yourself?" Young Mack smiled at the extra attention the other waiters and waitresses were giving him.

"Mackentosh Miller the second!" the pretty lady beside them spoke up and his suspicions were confirmed. He smiled from ear to ear as he looked her over.

"I'm sorry, do I know you?" Young Mack replied jokingly.

"By the way, we just followed *her* over here. I hope she's your sister or some close relative you haven't mentioned." Ambrea said with attitude.

"Why don't you go have a seat while I order something to drink, you want something?" The look on his face said more than his words, and she knew that he meant business. She wasn't tryna make him mad when she spoke up; he was already going through enough as it was.

"My apologies, I'll go wait over there and I'll have whatever you're having," Ambrea checked herself.

She was more than aware of the type of relationship she shared with Young Mack. Seventy percent was business, twenty percent was convenience, and ten percent was personal. The love was there but they had lines drawn, and most times she hated herself for drawing them.

"Wife?"

"Aeriella Garcia, you've finally gotten darker," Young Mack smiled, purposely ignoring her question.

"You still got jokes I see, what has it been—"

"Fourteen years," he interjected.

"Damn, you keep up with how long you haven't seen me?" Aeriella asked, more shocked than surprised.

"Nawl, I just remember the last time I did see you, that's all." She playfully bumped him with her hip, and they shared a laugh.

Ambrea wasn't feeling the friendliness between Young Mack and the mystery chick. She sat there eyeing them closely, but deep down she knew Young Mack and she knew he wouldn't purposely disrespect her, at least she hoped he wouldn't.

"You've grown, Young Mack," Aeriella said, stepping back to admire him.

"One could say the same about you, but what happened to your body?" he asked with his lips turned up.

"Wh-what do you mean what happened to my body?" she replied, a bit on the self-conscious side.

"Yo boobs are bigger and yo ass is so fat it looks like it need shoulder straps to hold it up," Young Mack joked but could not help but notice the ways she had changed and how much he liked her new look.

"Get the hell outta here," she laughed before playfully punching his shoulder.

"I see you been working out too," he continued to make her laugh.

"Damn, I haven't laughed this much in ages," Aeriella said.

"Should come around more often than every fourteen years," Young Mack stated as he looked her in the eyes. It had been a very long time since he last saw her, and he missed her more than he was willing to let her know.

"Are you gonna introduce me to her?" Aeriella could feel Ambrea grilling her as she talked with Young Mack.

Young Mack caught the looks coming from Ambrea, and immediately felt like an ass for ignoring her. He walked over and sat beside her. Aeriella watched the soft-spoken exchange of words between the two of them before the woman Young Mack had still not introduced her to looked her in the eye again, this time without any sign of aggression.

"Hi, I'm Ambrea," she spoke as she stood with her hand extended.

"Aeriella Garcia." Ambrea nodded as they shook hands before politely taking their seats. Aeriella caught the slick way Ambrea took Young Mack's hand inside of hers before placing them both in her lap. She smiled at how territorial Ambrea was acting over him.

"What have you been up to, A? Fourteen years is a helluva long time, ma," Young Mack said, placing his hands together atop of the table between them as he listened to her.

"Where do I start?" Aeriella sighed, thinking back on all those years.

"From the last time I saw you," he stated seriously. She could see it in his eyes just how serious he was.

"I don't wanna bore you, so I'll just sum it all up for you the best that I can remember things."

"I'll take it," he smiled and sat back.

"Shortly after graduation I attended Harvard School of Law, did my thing there, climbed the ladder in the system and became the youngest district attorney for the state of Georgia in history."

"Congratulations on that," Young Mack laughed. He was truly proud of her for following her dreams no matter how much grief he gave her about it fourteen years ago.

"Thanks, but years later I am now a criminal defense attorney in Georgia helping the thousands of people getting railroaded by the politics of the system. Being that I know how the wheels turn for the state, I also have the best advised strategies for my clients, both paid and court appointed. I love to help them protect themselves against the crooked courts and choose what's best for them."

Young Mack was in awe as he stared at the first girl he ever loved from across their small table.

"What?" Aeriella asked Young Mack as the young waiter from earlier stopped by and handed them their drinks.

"Thanks, homey, here, take that beautiful woman of yours out somewhere real nice," Young Mack stated and gave him a three-hundred-dollar tip.

"That's why I fuck with you the long way, Young Mack. I owe you for this one because baby been asking mad questions about going somewhere with just the two of us." Young Mack nodded his approval and shook hands with the guy before he stepped away happy as hell.

"Well, aren't you Santa's little helper," Aeriella joked and got a laugh outta Ambrea.

"I just love helpin' people, I guess we're not that different from each other."

"I bet," Aeriella said as she realized just how grown and sexy as hell he turned out to be. When they were younger, she'd always catch butterflies every time they were alone together, and she could feel them all over again as they looked into each other's soul.

"What has Mackentosh junior been up to all these years?" Aeriella questioned before taking a sip from her favorite drink.

"Apple didn't fall too far from the tree, A," Young Mack stated, being totally honest. She understood exactly what he meant, and her thoughts instantly moved to his father, a second father to her from her childhood growing up with Young Mack.

"How's he doing?"

"Up to our heads in attorney fees still fighting for his chance to appeal."

"Appeal?" Aeriella wasn't aware of Mr. Mack's request for an appeal. She had kept close ties to his case from Georgia. It wasn't like his case wasn't over every news channel in the United States during his trials.

"Yeah, pops found some serious holes in his case over the years and we're now ready to go full throttle on this appeal."

"And what's the hold up?"

"These money-hungry attorneys keep coming up with extra fees and excuses as to why they're afraid to accept his case," Young Mack explained.

"Afraid to take his case, why?" Aeriella asked curiously.

"You know the entire force came after pops. He even made some people's careers with his guilty verdict and sentencing."

"Still no reason to be afraid to accept his case," she strongly admitted.

"Same as we thought, but it's still a work in progress." Young Mack closed the top of his drink. He wasn't in the mood for it after thinking about his father.

"Here's my card, have him call me and I'll answer at any time, collect and all." She even wrote her personal number on the back of her business card to be sure that he could reach her.

Young Mack looked the card over before putting it away. He would be sure to give it to his father, but even he thought about reaching out to her personally.

"Well, I guess I should be going. Mom and dad are waiting for me to arrive."

"Give them my best wishes," Young Mack said as he stood after her.

"Nice meeting you, Ambrea," Aeriella extended her hand.

"Likewise," Ambrea said and shook her hand with a polite smile.

"I'll send your wishes, but don't be a stranger, Mackentosh Miller the second," she smiled while stepping into his warm embrace. She inhaled his strong Gucci cologne and enjoyed his firmness.

"Will do," Young Mack replied as he too enjoyed the feel of her tucked in his arms.

"Bye!" Aeriella waved as she walked away with Young Mack admiring her ass. She blushed from the way his eyes ate at her.

Young Mack was still in a trance, hours after running into his childhood love. Ambrea was rocking beside him as they made rounds delivering the shoe boxes he'd prepared prior to them going to the Galleria. Thought after thought of her ran rapidly through his mind. What were the odds of her showing up and being exactly what his pops needed after all these years! He made a mental note to call her as soon as he was alone.

"You good?" Ambrea asked as he drove through the city in silence.

"I'm good, ma," Young Mack looked at her with a smile.

"You haven't said much of anything since we left the mall," she pointed out.

"Still thinking about my mom a little bit," he half lied, knowing she'd buy it.

"I'm sorry if I stirred any bad feelings earlier. You just don't talk much about your parents at all."

"Yeah, I know," he replied.

"Why not, though they're a part of you!" Young Mack thought hard before saying anything further.

"My mom is sick, Ambrea, and the only thing that can help her is my father." Ambrea sat confused by his last statement, that was until it finally registered in her brain.

"I'm sorry to hear that," she apologized sincerely.

"We'll get her right, no worries there, or I'll die try-ing." Young Mack saw his phone vibrating on the middle console, and had forgot all about Ash calling him earlier.

"Talk to me, Ash," he answered and signaled for Am-brea to remain silent.

"We got a big fuckin' problem!" Ash yelled frantically over the phone.

"Whoa, state the business," Young Mack offered his undivided attention.

"Long story, we need to talk face to face like yester-day!" Ash stated.

Young Mack took one look at Ambrea and knew he couldn't show up with her. No one could know about their relationship. The coke connect would surely cut all ties with him and probably issue a death warrant on her for betraying him.

"Where are you?" Young Mack asked as he headed for his crib.

"Pink store on McGowan," Ash replied.

"I'm in route," Young Mack ended their call.

Chapter Nine

"They took you away from me," Phatts cried out over the body of his dead son. The feeling of losing his son was one next to losing himself, and the pain was indescribable.

Not many have survived the blast from an AK-47, and his son fought long and hard to live through it. Five shots riddled his body that night, and his final resting moment had come as darkness took him.

Mary was Phatts' wife, and she couldn't take seeing their son lying lifeless on the cold steel table which the hospital's morgue used to drain his body of fluids. Phatts had her taken home and assigned two of his most fearless men to guard her and never leave her side. The city was about to feel his wrath like never before as he hunted every single individual involved in the murder of his son.

Hurt and sickened to his core, Phatts backed away from his son's body while storing his resting image into his memory. After leaving the cold room, he never looked back as tears streamed his face. He handled things with his son's personal belongings and filed the necessary paperwork for the release of his son's body to a trusted friend who would handle everything from there until he put his flesh and blood six feet under the earth. The thought alone made Phatts wanna explode and get on some kamikaze shit, but he knew he had to keep shit together and find the persons responsible for his pain. He wasn't gonna rest until he avenged his son.

Phatts sat pensively, seething in the back of his new Bentley, scrolling through his son's call log and messages. Nothing stood out. Word about that night was already going around the hood, and the news of his son being a part of a dice game that ended his life was heartbreaking. He did his best to spoil him rotten and to show him that he never needed to be in the streets; now he couldn't even chastise him because someone had taken him away. The sound of his phone ringing brought his thoughts away from the gruesome visual of torturing his son's murderer.

"Yeah."

"We been putting pressure on the streets and I think we finally found something solid," Skooby said on the other end of their call.

"And where are you?" Phatts sat up, eager for this good news.

"Tha Brickz."

***

"How da fuck y'all end up in bed with this clown ass nigga, Ash?" Young Mack was furious.

"Rob got tired of waiting on you to give us something to do. He found someone who pointed him somewhere, who must've pointed him somewhere else and I guess he got in contact with Phatts to get the job. We never expected this," Ash frantically paced back and forth. Young Mack couldn't believe their luck and how shit was playing out. This was definitely some shit he could do without.

"Where is Rob right now?" Young Mack asked. He needed to talk to him and find out all he could about their situation.

"He's out there somewhere searching for Max. Max really shitted on us the hard way," Ash admitted.

"What was the take on this one?"

"Seven large!" Just the mention of the money made Ashton sweat even harder. "We got away with the bread but Max ditched us big time."

"Calm down so I can think," Young Mack really couldn't   believe   this   shit. "Lay low for a few days. I gotta go see my pops and get a grip on this Phatts nigga." Young Mack hopped into his whip and peeled out leaving Ash to his own thoughts.

"Fuck!" Ash yelled as he too hopped into his whip and pulled out.

***

Phatts accepted all the love he got from the hood as he walked through the Cuney Homes projects. It was his son's place of business. The love he had showed from every building and walkway around the projects. He spotted Skooby and immediately made his way over to where they stood. After embracing each other, Skooby explained what they had before opening the apartment door and allowing Phatts to enter with him on his heels.

"Phatts, salute OG," a raspy voice was heard through the dead silence once Phatts came into view of everyone inside of the small, crowded living room.

"Respect, young blood," Phatts patted the injured guy's leg as he sat deathly still in the medical chair.

Gangsta was his name, and he'd suffered a shot in the back from a shotgun blast the night Phatts son was killed. Barely making it away with his life, he was now paralyzed on the entire right side of his body. Phatts felt for the youngster but he was still alive and his son wasn't, so fuck him, he just wanted to know what happened with his boy and possibly find out who did it.

"What can you tell me about the night of the shooting?" Phatts asked after calming himself.

"Shit went brazy outta nowhere—" Gangsta started but got cut short.

"What the hell is *brazy?*" Phatts asked, confused as shit.

"It means crazy," Gangsta's brother—PJ—stated with respect.

"Go on," Phatts nodded.

98

"Shit just went br-crazy outta nowhere and nobody saw that shit coming. Five niggas approached that dice game and one of 'em knocked Malli's head clean off his shoulders," Gangsta teared up from the gruesome memory of his homeboy's murder.

"Take yo time, young blood," Phatts tried his best to sympathize with the injured young man.

"Niggas was asking us about their spot getting hit down on Canfield and Dennis, but nobody knew nothing about that shit and even if they did, how a nigga expect another nigga in these streets to snitch on some shit—"

"Hold up, did you just say Canfield and Dennis?" Phatts cut him off.

"Yeah, that's them nigga's words," Gangsta confirmed.

"Say less," Phatts stated and stood to his feet.

"Get you some rest, young blood. The rest of y'all get in the streets, but stay outta my way on this one. I know y'all wanna revenge these fallen soldiers, but Phatts got it, that's on me!" Phatts promised before leaving.

"Skooby, you know what that means?" Phatts asked as they made it to his ride.

"Talk to me," Skooby replied but he already knew where he was taking this conversation.

"We hit them and left someone alive and now it done came back to bite me in the ass."

Skooby couldn't think of any soothing words to tell his oldest friend and mentor. He was absolutely right. He looked over at Phatts, but Phatts didn't look back; he just stared at the world moving past them outside the car's window.

"We'll make 'em pay, you know my get down!" Skooby swore, and meant every word.

***

"Let me guess, you're here to see Mackentosh Miller," a sweet older woman spoke to Young Mack as he stepped up next in line. He'd taken the first flight out to Georgia to see his pops.

"Yes, ma'am, how are you this evening?" Young Mack flashed her his white-toothed smile.

"Wheeww, you even have manners like him. I'm fine, young man, boy, I wish my daughter could pick 'em like you. Handsome, well dressed and well mannered, boy, you sure are something." The woman smiled while handing him his visitor's pass. Young Mack thanked her before accepting his pass and moving along to the visitation area.

He could never get used to the visitation process that came along with visiting his father. The place was packed with visits all around when he stepped inside. He took his seat and waited for his father with a heavy state of mind.

"You're troubled, son, what's wrong?" Mr. Mackmillions said as he took a seat. Young Mack was so deep in thought that he hadn't even noticed his father enter the room.

"Am I that transparent?" Young Mack asked, looking his father in the eyes.

"I made you and I raised you, I know when something is weighing heavy on you. Stain my brain, son, what's going on?" He was always good at reading his son.

"My crew did the dumbest shit ever! They linked up with Phatts for a job—"

"Wait. They did what?"

"That's not even the crazy part," Young Mack admitted.

"What could be more crazy than pulling jobs for the same dude that got off on us, huh?" Young Mack shook his head because he knew his pops was fried the fuck out.

"They got off with seven large—"

"Seven large!" Mr. Mackmillions raised his eyebrows.

"Let me finish, pop." Young Mack understood how his pops was feeling but only if he knew what was coming next. He shook his head and continued.

"One of the guys they took on the job skated with the whole win, and now my guys can't find him."

Mr. Mackmillions had heard it all. He couldn't believe the guts of these young cats growing up in the streets without any loyalty. How could you get invited on a job then try to skate with the bag like a muthafucka wasn't gonna come hunting that ass down. The thought of that shit heated Mr. Mackmillions to his very core. He hated a greedy person.

"What's his name?" Mr. Mack wasn't fazed by the runner; he knew that his people could find nearly anyone living anywhere.

"His name is Max and he's originally from DTA."

"I'll have his info sent to you before your feet hit the ground in Houston tonight."

"You sure?" Young Mack asked curiously.

"What have I ever lied to you about?"

"Nothing, ever."

"That's right." Mr. Mack smiled, feeling as confident as ever.

"Don't sweat anything just yet though," Mr. Mack said as he watched his son's mood lighten. "Your friends should have a window to get that money back for now."

"How's that?"

"Phatts' son was gunned down in a dice game along with five others. One survived though, so I'm sure Phatts won't sit down until he avenges his son's death, especially after my source found out it was a retaliation from one of his father's hits. Hell, Phatts didn't even answer my calls when I reached out, and that's saying something."

Young Mack's face drained after hearing the news from his father. *One survived*—his mind replayed that statement over and over again as his father talked. "One survived," he said to himself.

"What's up, son? You got that look," Mr. Mack said, bringing him back to reality.

"Pops, I gotta bounce!" Young Mack quickly jumped to his feet.

"Sit down!" Mr. Mack read between the lines of everything going on.

"You don't understand, pops, I gotta get to my guys."

"No, I understand completely, now sit yo ass down!" Young Mack felt ashamed; his father had never cursed at him.

"Y'all out there fuckin' up tremendously and I'm not here for that, do you hear me!" Mr. Mack over stood his son's situation, and he knew that he couldn't be mad at a grown man for defending what was his. Hell, as far as he saw it, he didn't expect to keep the beast in his son for as long as he had, and now that it was surfacing, all he hoped to do was keep him contained.

"I got you, pop," Young Mack replied, feeling defeated.

"I'll get you the info on this one too, don't slip, son! Damn it, don't you fuckin' slip!" Mr. Mack could feel the rise in his blood pressure as he thought about the dangers of his son going up against a veteran like Phatts.

"I won't, I promise. Get me ahead on this and I'll come out on top, that's my word!" Young Mack vowed.

"This is a zero tolerance league, son, slippers count on all levels. The smallest slip will get you either killed or a life in here with me!" Mr. Mack jeweled.

"I got you."

"What were you thinking?"

"I'm out here, pops! I can't allow mufuckas to keep trying to shit on me and my team. I did it your way and fell back and now look at the shit my crew is mixed up in all because I haven't had any work for them. Niggas crossed the line on the wrong side of my hustles, pop, and for that they get laid down for that long nap." Young Mack spoke like the true game he was.

"Surely my blood runs through those thick veins in you," Mr. Mackmillions reflected. "I was talking about you not making sure that your targets were all done for. Never leave a mu'fucka breathing to tell on you or worse, come back to kill you. I'll lose my fuckin' marbles if something like that happened to you!" Mr. Mack admitted.

"I know you would, pops."

"My situation has to be put on the back burner for now until you get this shit under control. Don't you fuckin' slip up out there. Now get up outta here and get your boys on point. Tell them to vest up because that nigga is definitely coming."

***

Young Mack couldn't believe they had slipped so badly. *How could one survive that assault*, he thought to himself as he drove from the airport into downtown Houston. He pressed the phone sign on his touch screen radio and voice-dialed K-dawg.

"Big dawg," K-dawg answered, sounding groggy. Before Young Mack could say anything to him, his line beeped. He looked at his radio and saw that his father had come through just as he said he would with the info he needed on the boy, Max. *Damn, he fast*, Young Mack thought to himself.

"Mack, you there?" K-dawg repeated for the second time.

"Yeah, I'm here. Look, we gotta shut the shop down—"

"What? Man, hell nawl, bruh, this spot been jumping like a grasshopper!"

"Shut shit down and get all the shooters together and meet me at the condo, I'll be there shortly." Young Mack ended their call to keep from hearing K-dawg complain about his decision to shut down.

Shit was crazy and they weren't yet prepared for the type of drama Phatts and his henchmen would definitely deliver. He also knew that they wouldn't stop until they got all parties involved with the murder of his son. And all parties were them!

He needed desperately to catch up with Rob and gravely deliver the information his pops had given him. Surprisingly though, Rob wasn't answering his phone still. He never went without his phone; Rob was a real social media junkie. After exiting the highway, Young Mack decided to pull up on Ashton at home since he was close by, and since he had nothing to do with the shooting, being there wouldn't prove dangerous at all.

He got out of his car and was greeted at the front door by Ambrea. "Damn, you sexy," he said as he approached her. Her sexiness nearly made him slip up and wrap her up in his arms, but hearing Ash's voice coming out from behind her snapped that thought.

"What's up? Did you find out anything?" Ash nervously wondered.

"Haven't been able to get Rob on the line, but I did get a location on Max and, hopefully, he still has the bread." Young Mack wanted desperately to help Ash and Rob get the money that ironically belonged to the same man that was about to come for their heads.

"Fuck if he don't! Rob or no Rob, we need to get to that address and get that money back!" Ash stated before leaving the door and returning with a small backpack in his hand.

"Let's go," Ash said as he walked right past Young Mack.

***

"Long time," Em heard Gator's deep baritone of a voice before she saw him standing there watching her.

She had been working diligently to get any information she could gather on Phatts that would help Young Mack and his crew and so far nothing had hopped into her hands.

"Same here, Gator, how you been down here?" Em replied respectfully.

Gator was one helluva name for the monster of a man standing before her. Everything about him frightened everyone. He wasn't pretty easy on the eye, especially with the women. His quiet attitude and killer instinct earned him his name. His legend lived through the hearts and minds of many on the streets. He was the boogeyman to most that didn't know him, and even more to those that did.

"Haven't had to kill anybody in a solid while, so I'd say I'm saved now." He laughed a dark haunted laugh that sent chills up her arms. He had a funny sense of humor, but she paid no mind to it.

"An old friend has requested this visit, being that he can't physically be here with you," Em explained as she took a seat in his Mafioso styled office. The lights were dim, almost nonexistent, and she could only make out his massive silhouette as he slowly moved to take a seat in his huge backed chair.

"So, ol' Mackmillions has finally come to collect, huh?" Em didn't know what that meant but she hoped things didn't get any creepier than they already were.

"I'm not sure but I'm here as a favor to him and he said you'd understand," she said honestly, just as Mackmillions had instructed her to. He rehearsed her entire conversation with her to keep her from becoming a victim to Gator who sometimes could not control his urges to kill.

"I do!" Gator replied and stood at a faster pace than he'd moved since she'd been there. His quick movements startled her, and a slight gasp left her lips.

"You have nothing to fear, you're here as a friend to one of my closest comrades." Gator lifted what was supposed to be his hands but looked more like shovels with fingers to her.

Em sat still while doing her best to compose herself as he moved to pour himself a drink. Hearing the glass touch his teeth while he drank spread the chills from her arms to all over her body. This guy was really starting to get to her, but she fought for control to keep from letting Mack down, both of them.

"What is it that Mack seeks?" Gator asked after a second drink and returning to his seat.

"Phatts," Em cut straight to it.

"Can't do," his voice said deep and meaningfully. She sensed something there that she never sensed anywhere else.

"Can't or you won't?" She had to ask.

"Can't. We have an agreement and he's never failed on his side of that agreement!" Gator explained.

"Protection," Em understood.

Gator shrugged at the mention of his arrangements with Phatts. Em couldn't believe that a man so feared in the streets was also fearful of something other than God.

"What if I told you he had an agreement with someone else but broke it by touching their family?" Em shot in the dark.

"That would be something that person would have to handle, assuming that information is true."

"What if it were your family he touched?" Mackmillions had revealed to her that Gator was actually his family, but neglected to love and respect his father's name. Gator's

106

father was nothing short of what Gator was today, but unfortunately his father had murdered his mother with his bare hands right before Gator's young child eyes. Gator's father and Mackmillions' father were the only children born to their generation of family.

Gator sat quietly while trying to process what she was saying to him. It had to be his cousin reaching out to him for her to know that information. No one alive and breathing knew anything about their family. He sat forward in his seat and stared hard at the beautiful woman before him, and decided to hear her out.

"Touching my family would be a very *very* stupid thing for any man to do," he replied to her question. His calmness was chilling.

"Phatts robbed Mackmillions' son, Young Mack, at gunpoint."

"Did he know it was his son?" Gator asked curiously because not even he was aware that Mackmillions had a son, especially not one that was in the game. He hoped for Phatts sake that he didn't know.

"Mack shares a son with Sylvia." That was definitely a bomb to Gator's ears.

How could that be? he thought to himself and sat back while registering that information. Mackmillions had a son by Phatt's ex-wife, which meant that Phatts knew who Mackmillions' son was beforehand. That was a big problem. Gator would do anything for Mackmillions.

Unbeknownst to the world, Mackmillions was the reason Gator never saw the inside of someone's jail or boy's institution, after killing his own father for murdering his mother. Had Mackmillions not been there to sacrifice his own freedom by staging the scene and getting rid of the murder weapon, it would've been the end of him, and people would've never known the name Gator.

"I still can't touch him," Gator's answer was solid.

"Oh, I can't believe this," Em was ready to snap off.

"Unless," Gator stated, garnering her attention once again.

"What—unless what?"

"He breaks our agreement. You know—like—somehow forgets that he has obligations. It's in our agreement to never forget under any circumstances that we have an agreement."

"That would be next to impossible," Em sighed.

"Not necessarily," Gator admitted and had her ears open.

"He's used to me coming to get it from him. I've sent someone his way for the last ten years, so let's say I'm not around to send someone this time, how would he then keep our agreement?"

Em's mind was a racing frenzy after hearing his compromise. She couldn't think of any wise reasons to keep him from picking up that money from Phatts, then all of a sudden something hit her.

"Ever flew on a plane before?" Her question was a weird one but he answered her anyway.

"No, I don't do public much, and the airports are too open. I have enemies no man on this earth wants to meet." He sounded totally honest.

"Airport won't be a problem," Em stated, and a smile appeared on her pretty face.

Chapter Ten

Young Mack and Ash idly sat parked up the block from the address where Max was supposed to be. For the past hour there had been no movements in or out of there, and Ash was getting tired of waiting. To make matters worse, Young Mack was becoming irritated because of his phone blowing up with call after call from K-dawg concerned about their latest move. Going back and forth over the situation was the furthest thing on his mind. Young Mack made the call to fall back, and that was that; he wasn't going back on his decision. After gathering his patience, Young Mack willed himself to send K-dawg a text telling him to fall back and stay out of sight for the time being.

"I know we're not just gonna sit here, are we?" Ash asked, all attitude. Young Mack looked over at his homeboy like he was crazy for talking to him like that, but the sight of the murder weapon in Ash's hand caught all of his attention before he could even utter a word.

"Where the hell did you get that!" Young Mack pointed. He was astonished by the customized AR-15 equipped with a shell catcher and a sixty-round drum. The folding stock was adjustable and made it look as if it came out of a game.

"I collect shit like this, you should see my closet." Ash laughed. *I might just do that*, Young Mack thought to himself.

Young Mack was speechless. He'd been sleeping on Ash the long way. Sitting there staring at the house up the street was now getting to him also, and he wondered if anyone was even living there. The house was tattered and worn from years of weather damage, and no one looked as if they cared to do anything about it. Young Mack reached beneath his seat and took out his Sig .40 caliber handgun and placed it on his lap.

"I'm ready when you are," Ash said as he watched Young Mack with his hand already on the door release.

"Fuck it, let's move. I got shit to do."

Young Mack and Ash walked side by side with their weapons concealed between them until they reached the house and made it up the worn out wooden steps. Both men tensed from the loud creaking sound the old wooden porch made as they slowly approached the front door.

Young Mack placed a finger to his lips, signaling for Ash not to make a move or sound. He could see through the screen door and noticed that someone had left the door cracked open. Every nerve in his system screamed for him to just turn around and leave but curiosity got the best of him, and he pushed forward, past the whining screen door and into the cold dimly lit house.

Ash kept close to Young Mack with his weapon trained ahead of them just like he remembered vividly from his trials in the war game, CALL OF DUTY. This time only the adrenaline rush wasn't from a vibrating game controller. The pounding heart he was hearing wasn't through the speakers of a television; this shit was real, and he had to will his feet forward to keep up with his best friend.

They made it through the dark living room and headed towards the light illuminating from what looked to be the kitchen. Suddenly, Ash jumped from the strong vibrations against his thigh, letting off a round into the ceiling of the old home. A hail of debris fell over them as Young Mack stared hard at him. It was his phone vibrating but his nerves were shot, and clearly his finger grew a mind of its own. Ash pulled his phone from his pocket and showed Young Mack the screen before he snatched it from him. Ash sighed once Young Mack answered the phone and put it to his ear instead of throwing it against the nearest wall.

110

"Fuck is yo problem, got us searching high and low for you?" Young Mack fired off with his voice barely above a whisper.

Ash tried to focus in on their conversation but immediately figured that the caller was Rob. After listening for a second and not being able to make out Rob's words, he became worried about the take money again.

"So you got the shit back, that's kool." Ash relaxed after hearing those words of confirmation.

Ash took a deep breath and exhaled while moving forward into the bright-lit kitchen. He nearly emptied everything from his already empty stomach after making that decision. Vomit threatened to escape his throat, simultaneously burning his nostrils as his eyes clamped shut in effort to block out the gruesome scene before him.

Max's tortured and mangled body sat deathly still in an upright position at the round wooden kitchen table. His head was almost double the size Ash remembered since the last time he saw him alive, and the gaping hole in his forehead was enough to send Ash dashing past Young Mack to get outside into some fresh air.

Young Mack received the news from Rob seconds before Ash cowardly rushed past him. He didn't need to see Max's dead body to know it was the frightening factor that set Ash off.

"You straight?" Young Mack mockingly smiled at Ash once he reached the car.

"I guess Rob got the money," Ash stated, looking outside through the passenger window.

"Guess so," Young Mack laughed.

Bok! Bok! Bok! Bok! Bok! Bok!

A voice rang out in the streets between shots: "Bitch ass niggas killed my brother!"

Young Mack dodged for cover on the inside of his Benz as bullets riddled the exterior. He wasn't sure which direction the shots were coming from, but he was sure that he wasn't armed anymore. The dive inside the car caused his gun to fall from his waist.

"Ash, did you get a look at where the shots coming from?" Young Mack yelled over the thunderous shots being fired at them.

"Yeah, straight ahead twelve o'clock sharp!" Ash yelled back, full of adrenaline and fearful excitement. Ash had found a low spot on the floor board right behind the engine of the vehicle, and he didn't plan on moving at all.

"Well, do something about it then."

"You're definitely a better shot then me!" Ash replied while using his left hand to pass Young Mack his weapon from where he sat balled up. Young Mack shook his head and took the weapon.

From the sounds of gunfire, he knew the shooter was out there alone. After taking a deep breath, he readied himself for the shooter to have to reload his weapon. The guy was an amateur, sending his shots through the high windshield and car motor.

Once the shots ceased, Young Mack sprang into action from the floorboard of the car just in time to catch the guy rounding the vehicle on his side. His first shot slammed into the guy high, sending a crimson mist up into the night air from the guy's shoulder. The shooter yelped in pain from the surprise return fire, and the impact of the round lodging in his shoulder shocked him even more. Young Mack wasn't sure if he should finish the guy off or not. He didn't even know who the guy was. They shared hard stares for a moment before the guy went for his weapon and Young Mack was forced to finish him. The power of the three-round burst knocked the guy off of his feet, sending his weapon sliding across the street.

Young Mack slowly stalked his way towards the downed shooter and watched as blood leaked from his mouth with his eyes still open. No life stared back through the portals of his soul, and Young Mack knew the guy was a goner. Sirens could be heard in the close distance, snapping Young Mack from the trance his kill had sucked him into. One look at his car and he knew that wasn't an option for escape; it was totaled. He immediately grabbed Ashton up and they got outta there together.

***

"We gotta keep applying pressure on these young cats out here if we're gonna find the niggas responsible," Skooby stated as he sat inside Phatts' office, cleaning his weapons.

Phatts sat behind his desk, listening to Skooby go on and on about the dead ends they kept running into trying to find his son's killers. His ears were open but his mind was elsewhere. He looked down at the thick brown envelope that rested there on his desk, and sweat instantly began to coat his bald head. Skooby felt the distance between them but refused to speak on it, being that he knew Phatts was going through a lot. He was really bringing the heat to the streets, yet he could not bring joy to Phatts in the form of the heads of his son's murderers.

Phatts stared at the frightening envelope, and the fact that it was still there on his desk staring back at him was even more of a horror. He wasn't sure what was going on but he was worried to the core. His heart rate escalated from the sound of the hidden door revolving, yet he hoped to resolve his fears of having what was in the envelope delivered. The sight of Rob deepened his stress while making him more nervous by the passing minutes.

"Shit was sweet, Phatts, but I had to wait for the cop heat in the streets to die down before I stepped back out with yo dough, ya feel me," Rob lied but was happy as shit to get Phatts his portion of the winnings.

"Sit the shit right here so I can count it," Skooby stated, giving Rob an unassuring eye.

He didn't sweat the static coming from Skooby one bit. The hardest part of his day was over now and all he wanted to do was find some bad bitch's pussy to climb in and relax. On top of that, he knew Skooby didn't like him or anyone for that matter; he silently wondered if the nigga even liked his own mother. The thought in itself made Rob chuckle a bit.

"Sum'n funny, lil' ol nigga?" Skooby grilled him.

"Nawl, killa, I just be in my own world sometimes, I'm a crack baby." Rob smiled, brushing off all the attitude coming his way.

Skooby took his time unloading stacks of money from the bag Rob had brought in. He removed the rubber bands from the bundles before running them through the machines to get an accurate count of what was there while taking note of every bill counted in his head.

"Everything good, big homey?" Rob asked after noticing how very distant Phatts seemed ever since he stepped into his office with his money.

"That money over there right?" Phatts asked, looking him in the eye.

"Absolutely or else I wouldn't be standing here before you," Rob replied with confidence. "Counted it twice by hand." He could not resist poking at Skooby's methods.

"Come here, sit down!" Phatts ordered, and Rob complied immediately. He sat in one of the two comfortable leather chairs across from Phatts and waited patiently for him to speak.

"I need you to run an errand for me. I need you to take this envelope and put it into the hands of any person you see at this address." Phatts took his time making sure the address was on point before handing Rob the package.

"You know I got you," Rob took the thick envelope and gauged its weight and firmness, and from the feel he knew there was money inside.

"Make sure to put that in the hands of someone inside and they'll know what to do with it."

Phatts was still unsure as to why the package hadn't been picked up on schedule like always. There was no way for it to be forgotten about, something had to be up, or maybe he was overthinking things; either way, he needed that money to be delivered one way or another.

"Youngsta?" Skooby called out after Rob before his hand reached the handle of the exit door.

"Yeah, what's up, killa?"

"Trap house off of Dennis and Canfield, know about it?" Skooby asked, hoping he'd be familiar with it.

"That's one of Mack's spots, why?" Rob hoped like hell that they weren't planning on hitting Young Mack's spot because he wouldn't be able to allow that. That was definitely a no-go.

Skooby couldn't believe his ears nor their luck. He looked over at Phatts who wore the same exact expression, and he knew shit was about to get real now.

"Wait a minute, come—sit down," Phatts waved him back to the seat he'd just got out of.

"You sure that's your boy's spot?" Phatts asked as his temp began to boil.

Rob realized at that moment that something was wrong. Why would Phatts insinuate that Young Mack was his homeboy? He never spoke of them being friends to anyone, and Phatts had just implied it.

"I mean I know the nigga, pulled a few jobs with him, but I wouldn't say that he was my homeboy," Rob lied, tryna gauge the direction the whole thing was going.

Phatts lowered his eyes into slits as he stared murderously at Rob. Unbeknownst to Rob, he had just told two lies too many.

"Tie his ass up, Skooby!" Phatts growled through clenched teeth. Skooby had already moved into position the second the first lie left his lips.

"Gotta dress this one up real nice, Phatts!" Skooby chuckled as he did what he was told. He was excited about the kill.

"First one always gotta be a statement, Skooby, you know that," Phatts said while rounding his desk, putting brass knuckles over his fist.

"I'm confused, what did I do, Phatts?"

Rob's question fell upon deaf ears. Perspiration dripped down Phatts' chin after the beating he put on Rob.

Rob was unrecognizable. His left eye was swollen shut and cut above the brow; so was the rest of his face. Skooby checked for a pulse after analyzing the damage done. Rob's pulse was weak, very faint but steady.

"What ya wanna do with him now?"

"Cut his ass up and dump him where the whole entire city can see him!" Phatts ordered.

"Say no more."

***

"Fuck that nigga, blood!" K-dawg was heated and itching to put his Draco pistol into play.

"I say we take it to the nigga instead of waiting for him to bring it to us," Deuce stated, giving his input.

Young Mack hated to admit it to himself but Deuce was right. If they stood the chance of winning this thing out, they would definitely have to take the fight to Phatts, but how and where?

"Even if we did decide to go at him, no one knows shit about this nigga. It's no secret that this nigga is on a higher level in the game with a longer track record and some vicious ass killers on payroll." Hog spoke as if he was reading Young Mack's mind.

Young Mack was thinking about all the things they had stacked against them. It was times like these that he really wished his father was home. He knew this feeling all too well but understood that with due time his pops would once again grace the streets of Houston. His father was his mentor and his role model, and the crooked ass cops in the city along with politicians and fearful comrades had worked together to frame him, and they were determined to reverse his father's sentence. He needed his father's resources if he wanted to top the whole Phatts ordeal.

"Everybody just fall back for a few days, I need to wrap my head around all that's going on around us before I make any calls on this," Young Mack spoke over his soldiers having group conversations around his spacious living area.

"Fall back?" Deuce clearly wasn't feeling that idea.

"Didn't you say that this nigga is gonna be coming for us? He won't be packing light," K-dawg could see the fire in Young Mack but he wasn't about to become a sitting duck.

"Fuck all that *fall back* shit, homie we need—"

"I said fall the fuck back, nigga, is yo big ass deaf or do I need to speak another language? I meant what the fuck I said!" Young Mack was in K-dawg's face so fast no one could have stopped him if his plan was to kill.

Young Mack knew what and who he was dealing with; he knew all about his young homey but he wasn't lacking from his hip nor his shoulders. He'd been training at the P.A.B.A professional boxing gym most of his life, mix that with a life in the streets, niggas ain't trying him where he was best.

"A'ight, enough smoke, you two," Deuce intervened.

"Y'all just calm down and let's think this shit through 'til we find the best way to get the best results. We a team, not each other's enemies!" Deuce added, trying to calm his hood brothers down.

"Don't ever buck up to me again, K-dawg. I love you like you came outta my mother and you a beast, but I won't hesitate to make an example outta you at the end of the day!" Young Mack confessed wholeheartedly.

"I know that, and that's on me big bro, I'm just heated about all this shit going on around us. It's fucking with the money and when shit fucks with the money it fucks with my mental, ya feel me!" K-dawg said, accepting his fault.

The entire room was filled with Young Mack's loyal and devoted street soldiers and lieutenants. Everyone was relying on him to make the decisions that would guide them through whatever storm that they were about to head into. He took a look around and realized that there wasn't a nervous face amongst them. His men and the few women on hand were everything he felt he needed beside him if he wanted to beat this thing with Phatts. The thought that everyone breathing in the room may not be breathing at the end of the war tugged at his heart strings. He looked everyone over once again, this time studying their eyes and their body language, and he realized that they already were aware of the fact that everyone might not make it through. They knew what was at stake and it caused him to think back to his first statement and the reason he chose to make that decision.

"Look, I know y'all are fully aware of what warring with Phatts means, and by that I mean that by looking around this room I know we're not gonna make it through this war without casualties," Young Mack paced the opened floor as he spoke; he had everyone's attention.

"I said fall back because it's a boss move, it's a boss's decision and I gotta protect this shit here with my all. I didn't' say that shit because I feel we aren't willing to take it to this nigga's throat full throttle. We need head space, information on this nigga and his operation, and we don't have that one bit, and for that reason we will never get ahead of him and his crew. It's like fighting a ghost and we all know this nigga's get down, so that can't go overlooked.

"That's right, we need intel!" K-dawg cosigned.

"I think I got a guy," Pooh extended his offer to help anyway he possibly could.

"Bring him in, let's find out what he can give us," Young Mack ordered.

"Me too, if I'm not mistaken, one of my girls works for him at some club he owns," Persia offered her help along with her man's.

"You two get busy—the rest of y'all use every contact or connect y'all have in these streets to get us intel on this nigga or any and every crew member you know he's tied to!" Young Mack stated, downing a shot of Hennessy on ice. The wheels were now in motion, and he liked that.

"Nobody gets to sleep until we have enough to go off of, so I suggest you power up any way you can, but no hard drugs. We need everyone focused and keeping a low profile because we don't know what this nigga knows or has on us."

Young Mack watched as his crew moved in haste to do as he commanded, and the feeling of leadership mixed with the Henny strengthened his pride.

"Still no words from Rob," Ashton stated once the room was cleared.

"I'm sure he'll hit us up once he finishes breaking bread with that clown y'all joined the circus with. Hopefully, he'll be able to give us some intel against this nigga." Young Mack hated the sour ass decision Rob made to pull off a hit for his now sworn enemy. He truly needed Rob there with them and was praying that he would be able to give an exact location on where to find Phatts.

"What if—"

"Stop worrying about that grown ass man," Young Mack cut Ash off. "He'll be here. Just have patience."

He realized how rude he must have sounded to Ash. He needed him to know that he wasn't forgetting about their side of his organization. Shit was just fucked up, and lives were hanging in the balance, lives that he wasn't tryna lose.

"Look, Ash."

"No, I get it," Ash cut him off this time.

"No, you don't," Young Mack stated, keeping his calm. He sighed from the stress hovering over him as he moved and took a seat next to Ash on his couch.

"There is no way for me to say that Rob is safe around that guy, but he chose to get in bed with him."

"Yeah, after you refused to give us jobs," Ash pointed out.

Young Mack realized the truth in that statement, but their jobs weren't ran through him; his father had all the control in that department, yet Ash was missing the point.

"We couldn't pull jobs, Ash. Understand that us getting hit wasn't some lucky jackboys coming up on a trap score. Them niggas that hit us were sitting on us for who knows how long. We can't allow for them to do that shit again and maybe kill us this time." Young Mack stood to get himself another drink.

Ash remained silent as the facts in what Young Mack had just said resonated in his head. He never thought Young Mack had a valid reason for them to sit back for a while. Now he understood that he was protecting them all along.

"Maybe if you would've been answering his calls, he'd know that too," Ash stated while texting Rob's phone again.

"I never ignored any of his calls before, why would I do that?" Young Mack was now confused with what Ashton was saying.

"Wait—so you m—oh, shiiit!" Ash slapped himself upside the head after realizing his fuck up.

"You never gave him my new number, did you?" Young Mack asked. Ash shook his head, by way of saying:

No. He forgot all about it and now realized how vital being on the same page with Young Mack really was.

***

Darkness surrounded him everywhere, and the stale smell of dirty laundry lingered heavily, mixed with the raw smell of blood in the small space Rob was trapped in. The hurt he felt was excruciating as flashes of him getting beaten in and out of consciousness crowded his rattled brain. He didn't know where he was or what had become of him since gaining his consciousness back, but wherever he was before felt a lot better than what he'd been thrown back into feeling.

He took some deep breaths, bypassing the strong odors while attempting to get his thoughts back in order. He felt around the small space he was crammed into, but there were things everywhere. He focused in on the faint sounds he could hear but he wasn't sure as to where they were coming from. He was in deep pain as he moved his hands around, feeling the space he was in. It took him only a minute to figure out that he was stuffed inside someone's car trunk. Panic started to set in as thoughts of himself being set on fire and burned alive quickly flooded his mind. He frantically felt around, looking for the release to the trunk from the inside, but he found nothing. He began to think back to figure out what made Phatts so mad, but even there he got nothing.

In his panicked state he continued to move around the trunk until his hand suddenly came in contact with something hard. After further examinations, he felt that he was holding the handle to a hydraulic car jack. Moving with fear-stricken determination, he turned on his side to get a better grip on the handle so that he could remove it. Lying there on his side, he could now feel something poking him in the hip and reached down to feel what it was. What he felt against his body made him do a double check to be sure that his mind wasn't playing tricks on him.

Indeed, his mind was intact as he felt that his gun was still on his hip. He silently thanked his lucky stars for giving him mercy. He kissed his blue steel .40 cal, and the memory of putting it there resurfaced.

Walking inside of Phatts' club with pride and grace after securing the bag for Max's greedy ass had him feeling good about himself, and the way he handled the Max situation. He locked eyes with the tatted beauty behind the bar, and she gave him a slight nod while serving one of the many customers. He moved through the crowded establishment, bumping shoulders and grinding past patrons standing around drinking and having a good time. Phatts had an erotic assortment of women working the club's floor. He made his way over to the bathroom, and was stopped short by the long line waiting to handle their business in the men's room. The fact that he'd gotten the bread back that was taken from their score had a big ass smile on his face, and nothing could wipe that off.

Within minutes, the long line had died down and he was the next person in line when he spotted the two-man crew that searched him last go round headed his way. He locked eyes with them, and they surely saw him, but Rob felt like he could handle anything at that moment. One of the men stepped to him with his hand out and at first thought, Rob thought the guy was requesting his weapon, but he quickly dismissed that due to the fact that he wasn't armed the first time he came through. Dude didn't know him well enough to assure that he'd be strapped this time.

The weight of the package inside of the bag he held explained what the bear of a man was requesting. Rob looked down at his hand before sizing dude up like he was crazy for even considering that he would give him the bag.

"Hand it over," the guy demanded.

"Nawl, I'm good, big boy, this package here goes in Phatts' hand and his hand only before it can be touched by anyone he chooses to let touch it," Rob replied, hoping dude wouldn't flex.

"Didn't he say hand the bag over?" The second of the two spoke up for his partner.

"Be cool, homey, I didn't mean no disrespect."

"Then hand the bag over!" the first guy said, growing irritated.

Rob did as they requested, watching closely as they inspected the contents of the bag, one after the other, before giving it back to him and allowing him to pass.

"Bet y'all ain't never touched bread that heavy, huh?" He mocked them as he hurried inside the men's bathroom before they could give chase.

The sound and movement of the car snapped him from his reverie. His pulse quickened and his heart felt like a bomb just before it was due to explode, then everything just stopped, including his breathing when he heard the trunk lock release its catch.

Chapter Eleven

The smoldering heat and the acrid smell of burning flesh inexorably threatened to suffocate Mackentosh "Mr. Mackmillions" as he aimlessly scoured along a thin path headed to a destination he could not see. He was lost, and finding his way through seemed almost impossible for him to do. Fear was an emotion that Mr. Mackmillions was unfamiliar with, but he felt kinda nervous by the raging fires roaring on either side of a path so thin that only his feet alone could move along it. Both sides of the path felt as if the fires were breathing and fighting in an attempt to consume his entire being just as the tormented individuals already there were writhing and screaming inaudibly. Their bodies living inside the flaming fires pleaded for the fires to release them as he looked on with an intensively unfamiliar feeling in the pit of his existence.

"Mack, help me, Mack!" one of the prisoners in the fire yelled out and he could hear his words as clear as anything.

"Aaarrgghh!" Mr. Mackmillions howled in agony from the sweltering feeling of his skin sizzling from the death grip of the person reaching out to him.

"We gotta get 'em, we gotta get 'em all for what they did to us." Mr. Mackmillions opened his eyes and stared at the tortured soul of a man whose loyalty he'd forever swore to.

"Max—that you, Max?"

"We gotta get 'em all, Mack!" The voice faded away as did the visual image along with the heat consuming his body. He could still see Max's soul reaching out to him as the images faded, but he could no longer hear him nor feel him either.

"Miller! Yo, Miller!" Mr. Mackmillions heard a voice different from that of his nightmare of a dream.

124

His sweat-drenched sheets clung to his chest and abs as small chill bumps spread throughout his body from the strong wind blowing from his clear prison fan. He simply embraced the cool air while using both hands to wipe his face free of perspiration caused by the extreme nervousness he felt in the depths of his nightmare. "Yo, Mack, you up, you got a visit," the voice spoke up again.

After gathering himself, he stretched and welcomed the tightness of his muscles from the maxed workout he completed the evening before his eyes shut and sleep found him. He swung his feet from the bed into the cold leather of his Virgil Abloh-inspired Louis Vuitton slippers. Moving sluggishly over to the all-in-one sink and toilet combination, he took care of his morning hygiene. Shortly after finishing his hygiene, he stretched some more, then took his time fitting into his starched down prison uniform. He carefully looked over his shoe collection, and decided on a pair of exclusive all white Jordan retro elevens, courtesy of his son. He laced his shoes and made his way to the officer's chambers to be searched.

He could already hear the noise coming from the visitation area as he was escorted down the long hallway. It was a noise he enjoyed hearing, a noise that brought him closer to his family, a noise that explained to him that love was real and no matter how much one hardened their heart, it would still remain.

"Mack, we got a situation," a high ranking official said as he approached them from up ahead.

"Situation like what?" Mackmillions calmly asked in his usual deep baritone voice. He was all business when it came to the officials and their officers.

"Nothing major. Can you step in here for a second and I'll fill you in, it'll only take a quick second," the ranking official stated while motioning for his escorts to stay outside.

Mackmillions took a long minute debating if he wanted to play the game with the ranking official before him. It was clear to him that something was up this guy's sleeve but he just wasn't sure as to what it was. He thought about all the things that he was involved in, and all of the latest beefs he'd been through along with his men, and nothing really stuck out to him to cause him to be leery of the man requesting his time. Mackmillions decided to hear the guy out instead of keeping his family waiting by dancing around with the guy, so they entered the room alone.

After stepping closer to the desk in the room, the ranking official tossed his paperwork down before turning on his heels to face Mr. Mackmillions.

"You have too many visitors here today," the man stated dryly.

"Too many visitors?" Mackmillions couldn't believe this guy was wasting his time. Time he could be spending with his family.

"Three adults with no kids," Mackmillions stood there gauging if this guy was serious. "This has never happened with you before, so I ask now, is there something going on that warrants you to be visited by three adults."

"I hope not, but nothing is too much to handle for me." Mackmillions confessed proudly.

"Sure there isn't. Okay, check this out," said the official whom Mackmillions had yet to learn his name. "Let's say I was to allow all three visitors, and say I tact on an extra hour due to a family emergency. Now let's say, hypothetically speaking, I need your sponsoring or backing, whatever you wanna call it, could I count on you to come through like everyone around here claims you could?"

"See now that depends," replied Mackmillions.

"On what?" the curious and desperate official asked.

"Whether you're genuinely in need of my backing or if you're tryna set me up on a bogus bribery charge in which I would hypothetically have to call my lawyer. He's my best clean-up guy." The official immediately caught the underlying threat in Mack's words.

It was known to everyone on the compound who Mr. Mack was, and how he and his team got down. He was serving a shit load of time, and freedom didn't seem promising and everyone knew that, so the mentioning of his lawyer was definitely a murder-for-hire situation.

"No funny shit here, Mack, here's the deal. I'm in over my head in debt with Mr. Vorhese over the Sicilian mafia or whatever's left of them, anyway." Mackmillions was very familiar with the name, but he wasn't fond of its existence. Vorhese moved like a mafia don of the 50's and 60's, and acted as if everything and everyone was beneath him and his goonies. Mackmillions couldn't stand the old fart, but he respected his business savvy and his old-fashioned brutality when it came to disloyalty.

"Overhead?" Mackmillions asked the ranking official.

"Five large," the guy said, and even the mentioning of the amount he owed brought perspiration to his lip and forehead.

"Too much for my taste, I'll just see my family at another time," Mackmillions stated and turned to leave.

"W-wait!" the official stated in panic mood. Mackmillions slowly turned back to face the desperate man. "What would it take? Man, I really need this." The dude was fanning himself with the paperwork for Mackmillions' visit.

Mackmillions stepped into visit feeling like a new being after finishing his business with the ranking official, Captain Isaac. With the captain in his pocket, he knew things would be on the up and up for him and his team from now on out. Looking around for his son and company, he got the shock of his life. Never in a day would he had ever imagined seeing them together, there at the same time. *What the hell*, he thought to himself as he willed his feet to keep moving.

Young Mack was the first to stand and hug his old man, followed by Em. There was a long and intense stare down between Mackmillions and his third visitor, and it was making Young Mack very uncomfortable. Young Mack was aware of who Em was to his father, but the monstrous man sitting quietly with the devil's eyes was very intimidating, and Young Mack wished for the second time that day that he'd made contacts to buy a pistol, or submarine missile, to take his big ass out.

The stare down washed away once Mackmillions blinked repeatedly. The monstrous man laughed a chilling laugh that got to Young Mack and probably every other person in the visitation room.

"Gator," Mackmillions stated.

"I'm still here, Mack," Gator replied while standing to embrace his only living relative besides the young man who he'd yet to meet there with them. Gator studied the young man ever since his eyes first saw him there waiting for them to exit their flight on the private air strip. He was the spitting image of Mackmillions and their father. He knew immediately that the young man was his cousin's offspring.

"Long time, big guy!" Mackmillions said once Gator released him from his huge arms. Mackmillions wasn't a small guy by any means but standing beside his cousin, Gator, he was that of a normal sized man to a giant. If there was any comparison to match it would be, Kyrie Irving to LeBron James.

"Yes, but it seems like time couldn't have done you any better," Gator smiled while looking over Mr. Mackmillions.

Mackmillions was more than happy, to say the least, that his only family was there together, but the sour expression on his son's face explained that they hadn't made the trip to see him together.

"Junior, this is someone I've been waiting to introduce you to for a very long time," Mackmillions stated. Young

Mack knew it had to be serious because that was the only time his father referred to him as 'Junior'. His father was well aware of how much it meant to him to earn his own name in a world living underneath his shadow, and he respected it one hundred percent.

"Son, meet our cousin, Gator. Gator, meet my son and only child, Young Mack—"

"Hold up—Gator, as in THE GATOR?" Young Mack asked as the terror behind the name threatened to make him back away.

"Don't believe the hype," Gator said, after smelling the fear permeating from Young Mack.

"Shiiiit—what you mean don't believe the hype, you mean the stories I've been hearing all these years aren't real?" Young Mack needed to know.

"No, they're real but the attention to them seems to heighten the way they really happened, you know how that goes."

Young Mack swallowed in disbelief.His head was spinning like crazy. He couldn't believe that he was blood relative to THE GATOR. Legend had it that Gator never left his compound—nicknamed by the streets as *The Swamp*—unless murder was his motive. Rumors had it that Gator took his time killing them, skinning many of his victims before feeding on their flesh and drinking their blood like wine. Young Mack wasn't a kid, so he could tell what was true and what was folklore, especially now that he was seated next to the man behind the legend in itself.

Mackmillions sat back and enjoyed it as his visit went on with his son drilling question after question about Gator's legend. Em sat there quietly stealing long glances at him while resting her right foot in his lap. He smiled while adjusting himself in his seat so that he could massage her aching foot.

"What about the church story?" Young Mack asked. He was intrigued by his cousin's resume. His legend would live on forever, and Young Mack was enjoying himself talking to him.

"A'ight, enough with the questioning me, your turn," Gator stated, then inquired about his situation with Phatts.

That got Mackmillions' attention as well, which halted the foot massage Em was definitely enjoying. Young Mack and his father alternated while explaining everything going on with them and Phatts in great detail. Gator's mind was made up before the explanations were complete, but he needed to hear them out. He was searching for every reason to go back on a promise he'd made where business was concerned. Money wasn't an issue. Gator had morale, and he always stood firm on his word no matter if it were client or coon.

Mackmillions was deep in thought when he sat back and noticed Gator's deadly eyes trapped in a direction beyond their table. He took the initiative to search out and find whatever it was Gator was so fixed on. Nothing seemed out of place in the large visitation area until something did, and Mackmillions took to the threat like sharks took to blood in the water. It irritated him that he was dictating the death of a thorn in his side while another one was growing yards away from where he sat.

"Problem?" Mackmillions asked Gator without turning away from the potential threat. Gator remained silent as Young Mack and Em both joined their stares.

Mackmillions was that nigga, in and outside of prison, and a muthafucka staring at him and his family was a definite no-no. Gator's heavy hand grabbed his shoulder just as he was about to stand and go over to address his uneasiness.

"How long have you known me?" Gator's question sounded silly and outta place but Mackmillions decided to humor him.

"Your entire life."

"Have I ever challenged you in anything?" Mackmillions didn't know if that was a trick question or not but he answered anyway.

"Yeah, I can recall a few times," Mackmillions reminisced.

"Well, I would never challenge him at anything," Gator confirmed. "Not unless my life depended on it," he added, thinking back to a time long ago when that statement first came to life.

Young Mack couldn't believe his ears, and neither could Em who sat there in awe. Mackmillions understood his cousin and knew that he was a junior master at life's big chess game. He held authority, but so did every other piece on the board because each piece was as deadly as the person moving them allowed them to be. For that reason alone, Mr. Mackmillions chose not to play the game but be the maker of the board and the person in control of each person moving the pieces. He accepted what his cousin was telling him and would use that knowledge to move in the future.

"He trained me to see at night," Gator's statement was more than Mackmillions imagined he'd say. He immediately understood what that meant.

Respect was due to anyone of that caliber. Most would fear a man that dangerous and with that much power, but not Mackmillions who understood their kind. Respect was all he had to give. When it came to life's deadly and treacherous ways, Mackmillions was the king of survival simply because he loved and respected the rules of nature.

"What's understood needs no explanation," Mackmillions confirmed, then turned back in his seat.

"What's good, pop?" Young Mack asked with flared nostrils.

"Nothing, son, just making plates up top, that's all." Mackmillions could see the worry in his son's eyes, and he checked it immediately.

"I'm still the same me as I was when I left the streets, son, don't ever forget that. You hear me?"

"That same fire that burns in here," Mackmillions reached out and touched his son's chest over his heart. "It started right here and it's still churning. I've learned to contain it but it's still there."

"One hunid, pops." Young Mack relaxed, knowing his pops was okay.

"Now let's get back to the Phatts ordeal," Mackmillions changed lanes.

"Don't worry, Mack, I'll handle it," Gator finally agreed.

"I know you will," Mackmillions replied and vowed no more business talk for the remainder of their visit.

***

"Shit!" Skooby gasped after opening the trunk of his Crown Victoria and getting the surprise of his life.

"Should've killed me earlier, bitch boy!" Rob growled as he climbed outta the car's trunk, grinding his teeth. The sight of Skooby made his chest burn with hate. Skooby never even gave him a chance as a hustler, and for that he would make him pay for every disrespectful thing he ever said to him.

Keeping his weapon trained on Skooby's heart, the chill of the night air gripped him, and he welcomed the cold feeling. The thick taste of blood in his mouth fueled him even more to punish the man before him.

"Turn around and get on your knees, mu'fucka," Rob ordered but Skooby failed to comply.

Boom!

"Aarrgghh, you pussy!" Skooby yelped in pain and instantly reached at his blown-out right knee. He remained standing in defiance and refused to go down.

132

"If you gone kill me, nigga, handle yo bidness, pussy!" Skooby howled through the pain he was feeling. The pain was overbearing, and had him saying shit he really didn't mean.

"Oh, you're gonna die, but on my terms, dick!" Rob mocked while relieving Skooby of his weapon.

Rob sat back against Skooby's trunk and got his head right. He wasn't sure how he was gonna head things from here. So many pieces were out of place that he didn't even know where to begin. One thing was for sure: he'd been beaten senseless because of something Young Mack did, and shit wasn't sitting right with him. He needed answers, and muthafuckas were about to come up off that shit real quick.

Boom! Boom!

Rob let his cannon rip Skooby's other knee apart, along with his right shoulder. He wasn't about to let up until he got what he needed outta him, and he was just getting started.

Chapter Twelve

Cameras flashed, and news stations reported as people observed the apprehension taking place at Houston's Hobby Airport. Sheriffs and investigators alike lined the entrance of the building in wait of what held everyone's attention.

Young Mack hated his luck when the bad news came crashing down on him. He was being read his rights and arrested for a double homicide. Onlookers hurled obscenities towards the officers who held Young Mack on both sides escorting him through the terminus. Young Mack watched as people recorded him taking his last steps to the many police cruisers on the other side of the glass doors ahead of him. He looked over his shoulder and watched as onlookers questioned the officers about arresting yet another black man in white America. He shook his head in disbelief and knew that the whole world would see footage of him being carted off in a matter of minutes.

He'd been in the streets putting in work, and this particular arrest was one for him to question if he'd spent his last day as a free man. His mind was heavily troubled but his heart was light after visiting with his father and getting to know his only known relative outside of his mother and father. He smiled to himself as the cops lowered his head and stuffed him inside an unmarked car.

The long ride to the precinct from the airport was a bumpy one, due to the hard ass plastic back seats and the officers' failure to slow the fuck down. Shit had Young Mack beefing like a mu'fucka. He couldn't understand how he allowed himself to slip up this bad. Shit was ugly, but he was ready to hear all evidence the investigators had against him. He wasn't saying a word until his lawyer was on payroll, so they could forget about that part of the investigation.

Processing was quick. He was mugshot, thumb-printed, read his rights again, and screened by the medical staff on hand. Shit was damn crazy, but he was built to withstand the pressure, so he endured it. After processing cleared him, the officers walked him to a holding cell there at the department until he saw the judge. He gagged from the raunchy smell in the empty cell. Rust stained the metal all around him, and the wet floor underneath the toilet reeked from the pungent odor of old piss. The blinking light up above the sink and toilet combination caused the small space to seem haunted, as if an evil spirit were trapped inside tryna escape the very place the officers left him to dwell in.

Being locked behind bars really bothered him to his core. He promised himself to hold court in the streets if this day was ever to come. He deemed it way more dignifying than losing his respect as a man being pushed around and ordered to do things he could not refuse to do without further punishment. Being fresh off a public flight handicapped him and zeroed his chances of doing just that. He had no fire-power to get shit popping, and he hated that.

Hours passed before sleep found him struggling with his thoughts. It didn't last long; guards came knocking on the bars in order to wake him. The loud clanking of the nightstick hitting against the metal bars was enough to wake the entire second level tier.

"Wh-what's good, man? A nigga tryna sleep, fuck!" Young Mack said, still groggy from the little sleep he did get in.

"Phone's open, new house, hope you got someone who'll accept it, it's collect," one of the two guards stated with a lame ass laugh.

"What's up with a toothbrush and some toothpaste?" Young Mack asked as he stepped outside of the cell.

"Should've gotten that in processing on your way in," the same officer stated. He had a thing against murder suspects and didn't care one bit if they were guilty or not.

"No one gave me shit! I'm in that stank mu'fucka assed out," Young Mack explained.

"I got chu, homey—after you're done with the jack, I'll go fetch something out for you," the black officer stated while looking his white partner dead in the eyes.

"Good lookin'," Young Mack stated, ignoring the tension between the two guards.

Young Mack stepped to the phone and dialed the first number that came to his mind, but no one answered. He cursed himself for living from his iPhone and having everyone's number saved under a name instead of by numbers. He dialed the second number and received the automatic operator saying he'd dialed an unworking number. Frustration began to set in as he stood there in deep thought, so deep that he'd actually come up with a number that he could never forget, especially being that he kept the bill paid up monthly without ever using it to talk to its owner. He kept it paid up due to an emergency, and this was one of those times it suited him best to use it instead of overlooking it. The line rang nearly five times, and just as he was about to hang up, someone answered it.

"Who the fuck is this calling my line collect? Bitch ain't made outta money. Who gone pay me for this shit, huh? I ain't that bitch, you hear me? I ain't that bi—"

"Ma," Young Mack spoke softly, interrupting her drug induced rant. He could tell from her random rambling that she was high.

"Ba-baby Mack?" she asked, utterly confused.

"Yeah, it's me, ma, how you doing?"

"Baby Mack, is this you? I hope like hell ain't nobody playin' no damn prank because I'ma fuck around and catch a body. I don't play 'bout my baby boy!"

"No prank, ma, it's really me," Young Mack confirmed, then listened to her dam break.

136

Her sobs brought tears to his eyes, but he collected himself and spoke lightly, informing her on all things going on with him before he explained what he needed from her.

"Moma on it, baby, you know I got you." She agreed.

"Cool, you be easy, ma, and I'll see you in a few days."

"Whatever you need and I can do, I got you."

"Talk to you later then, ma, I gotta go." Young Mack hated to hear his mother so lost and away from her old self. It pained him so much, and he knew there was nothing he could do for her until she was ready, and he wished for that every day he thought about her.

"Baby Mack, someone came to see me the other day, guess who it was, baby? It was Aeriella. We talked about you for hours, Baby Mack, and I told her she still loved you and you still loved her," Sylvia laughed.

"Ma, you can't go telling her things like that, we're not kids anymore," Young Mack was playing himself. The thought of Aeriella made him smile one of those childhood crush smiles.

"I understand, son. I just wanted to let you know that I saw her. She's beautiful, baby, you should marry her. Surely I'd get myself to welcome good-looking grandkids." She chuckled. She was high as a kite, but happy as hell to hear from her only child.

"Ma!" Young Mack laughed because she was pushing it.

Hearing her laugh on the other end made him wish he could see her. He could feel the joy in his mother's words.

"You know, maybe you should call her to help you on this one. I don't need to be in a position that'll only make you hate me more than you already do." Her words shocked and caught him off guard; they nearly knocked the wind from his lungs.

"I don't hate you, don't think like that!"

"Yeah, right, baby Mack, then why haven't I seen you in so long, huh?" It's been years since I've held you in my arms!" Sylvia stated as she began to cry again.

"That may be true, but I see you all the time and as long as I know you're good then I'm good, ma."

"I hear you, but even I hate me now too, but not enough to do my son dirty. I'll contact Aeriella and have her make these moves for you. I don't need to have access to anything my sickness will cause me to destroy."

Young Mack loved his mother's loyalty; he valued it because people weren't made like that anymore. Everywhere you looked, someone was trying to get over on something or another. He'd given her his address and the code to his safe, which held hundreds of thousands of dollars and kilos of coke, but she refused to go there and ruin everything. Refused to steal from her son, knowing she wasn't strong enough with her addictions to handle all that was there.

After spending time talking to his mom, he knew some things had to change in his life. Moving around in the small cell was starting to get to him, so he brushed his teeth and got back in his rusted metal bunk with thoughts of his sick mother flooding his mind, while thoughts of Aeriella and him growing up loving one another threatened to take over. He rolled over on his back and stared at the graffiti-tagged ceiling. He shook his head after recognizing a few names here and there before his eyes became heavy, and sleep found him once again.

***

"Fuck!" Mackmillions yelled out as the news of his son's arrest hit him. "Double murder?" he asked himself as he paced his cell. He knew his son was out there living his life, but to slip up on anything this major was a definite no-no. Mackmillions was not prepared for some shit like this to happen, not at a time like now. Things were beginning to look good for him due to the help he was receiving from the unit's captain. He was having all of his records pulled, dating back to his trial and first days of incarceration in federal prison. He knew there was evidence there to award him a new trial and a possible release after the appeal process was over. Young Mack getting knocked hurt him and it would cost time, money and resources to ensure that he kept his freedom, and Mackmillions was prepared to give up everything he owned to make sure that happened, even if it meant he'd have to start anew.

"Yo, Mack, you got a couple of visitors on the block," Cook announced, hoping not to get yelled at for bothering him.

Mackmillions respected Cook on a level many others never reached with him in life. Cook had proven to him that there was nothing he wouldn't get involved in with or for their cause, and that cause being to get Mackmillions back on the streets with hopes that he'd soon follow after Mackmillions got himself together as a free man.

"Who is it?" Mack asked, now facing Cook.

"Cats from the east coast, Mexican guy and a white guy," Cook replied, ready to pop shit if it were his orders.

Mackmillions took his time approaching the two men there to see him. He was being flanked by Cook and joined by Del, Cook's bloodthirsty hitman. Del's reputation was known and respected by many, so niggas thought twice before even speaking to the mad man. Mack stood face to face with the heavily tattooed Mexican guy. He could tell they were fit and probably ready for anything coming their way, but the hurt he'd put on them would be nothing like anyone had ever seen if anything felt off about their visit.

"I don't' know either of you, so why are you here and it better be good!" Mackmillions crossed his arms over his chest and stared into the eyes of the man before him.

"My boss wants to meet with you," the tattooed guy spoke up for the two.

"And that is?" Mackmillions asked, already knowing this would pass.

"We don't say his name. We only speak his orders."

"His orders? Okay, go tell your boss that if he wanted to speak with me he should have showed his face and not sent his flunkies to summon someone of my caliber!" Mack stated and turned to walk away.

"Do understand that he knew you'd say that so he welcomed himself," the white guy said before bowing in unison with his partner and disappearing the same way they came.

"What was that about?" Cook asked as they walked with Mack back to his cell.

Mackmillions shrugged because he couldn't be sure, but he had a good feeling that it was the same guy from the visit that Gator warned him about.

"Mackentosh Miller," a raspy voice spoke from the darkened corner of Mack's cell. The voice in itself was chilling but the presence of another person in his cell brought chills to all of them; surely this person was crazy as hell.

"Who the fu—how the hell did you get in here?" Mackmillions staggered.

"We must speak in private," the voice spoke again.

"Ask your men to step out," the voice warned.

"Who are you?" Mackmillions asked, ignoring the potential threat.

Thud! Thud!

Mackmillions gasped when his men hit the floor in a heap, one on top of the other.

"They're just sleeping, only because I came in peace. Not many men in life, dead or alive, can swear to have witnessed that." The voice spoke calmly before the person behind it revealed himself.

140

"You!" Mackmillions gritted his teeth in anger.

"Yeah, me, but be warned, Mackentosh, I only come in peace." Mackmillions looked at the bodies of his downed men, and his hands instantly balled into fists. Gator had warned him about the man before him, so he already knew this guy wasn't a joke.

"What do you want?" Mack asked irately.

"We both know the answer to that and you're my only way of getting it."

"Nawl, that ain't happening." Mack would give him his life before he betrayed his blood relative.

"I come in peace, Mackentosh," the guy persisted.

"You keep saying my name as if we're familiar, yet I have trouble remembering yours."

"My name is Ramone Ali Talib. My students and others call me Shadow. Be warned to never use either unless death is your intention. Life is all about intentions, Mackentosh."

"So what are yours with Gator?" Mack curiously questioned.

"Never in life have I trained anyone as uniquely skilled and as special as him. He's my star pupil and I have work for him, highly profitable work, might I add, something that could not only guarantee my freedom but yours as well."

"At what costs?"

"He'll know as soon as you speak with him," Shadow spoke while stepping back into the darkened corner and outta sight.

"What the fuck just happened?" Cook stated, and Mackmillions turned to look at his dazed partner. Del came to immediately after hearing Cook's voice, and on high alert.

Mackmillions slowly stepped into the dark corner in hopes of feeling a man of any kind standing there with them, but there was nothing, not even a piece of clothing.

"I don't know but it's some freaky shit in the air," Mack stated after checking the empty corner.

***

"Baby—bae, someone's at the door." Mary spoke in a groggy voice after being awakened by a loud pounding at her front door. She shook her husband time after time in an attempt to wake him enough to go and answer for whomever was there.

"Grrr-where's Monica?" He spoke with clear agitation in his voice.

"It's four in the morning. She leaves at two and if your butt would spend more time at home than in the streets you'd know that." Mary provoked him as she swung her feet from their bed and into her comfortable house slippers.

The loud snoring coming from next to her let her know that she was on her own and out of an argument. It crossed her mind that whoever it was beating at that time of morning was about to be in for a rude awakening, something she hadn't had to do in over a year. She chuckled as she thought back on how surprised the rude young lady at the office was when she popped off and went straight hood on her. The thought of going back to that saved the person at the door because it was something she did not wanna do.

She calmly made her way down the stairs and into the foyer before clasping her robe ties and bringing them together in a tight knot in front of her. After getting herself together, she leaned against the door on her tiptoes, and took a look through the peephole but saw nothing. She reached along the wall beside the door and flipped on the porch light and lit the entire area in front of her home but still saw nothing there.

She looked around the yard for a second, then killed the light and turned on her heels and headed back to bed, exhausted. She hated having to use the stairs to get back to bed, but she loved the layout of their home, especially since she designed it herself.

Boom! Boom! Boom! Boom! Boom!

Mary flinched from the intensity of the loud knocks against the front door. She paused for a moment and looked towards her bedroom, where her body ached to be. The knocks on the door sounded again, just as intense as the ones before, and before she even realized it, her feet were carrying her back down the stairs and further away from the comforts of her bed.

"Who is it!" she asked before checking the peephole once again.

"It's me, Mary!" Skooby's troubled voice sounded.

She could clearly see that he was wounded and covered in a lot of blood. Seeing all that blood spiked her heart rate and caused her hands to shake uncontrollably.

"Oh my god!" Mary damn near choked from the sight of Skooby, who was being held up by the shoulders of a young man she could not see clearly.

Fear put her in autopilot, so much so, she never noticed the scowl plastered on the face of the young guy supporting Skooby's badly damaged body. She fumbled with the deadbolt lock because of the severe shaking, but managed to get the lock opened, and she immediately felt the weight of Skooby's body as it forced the door opened. His head hit the ground in the foyer with a thud.

She gasped and hurried down to aid Skooby who was in very bad shape. His blood pooled the floor as he laid there unconscious.

"What happened to him?" she asked in a panicked tone.

"I happened," Rob stated with his weapon trained on her head, ready to take her life.

He hesitated after seeing the look in her eyes. It wasn't a look of disgust, a look of fear or disdain, no, it was one of extreme familiarity. Something so familiar it gave him chills as he stared back into her light brown eyes. Her eyes never wavered as death looked down on her, but they filled with tears as she continued to gaze deep into his portals of life in disbelief.

"Mary-what the fu—" Rob heard that dreadful voice and shook his vision clear of the familiar woman and went into kill mode.

"Fuck you, nigga!" Rob yelled while firing away at Phatts at the top of the stairs. Phatts retreated in haste for cover as bullets riddled the wall where he once stood.

Fragments of wood and sheetrock exploded as Rob let loose with his cannon in a blind-eyed fury. He needed to end Phatts before he ended up losing his life behind something he had no knowledge of. Phatts had issued his death sentence once, and he'd be damned if he'd allow it to happen again.

"Stooop!" Mary yelled like a woman possessed. She was sick and tired of the death hovering around her.

"On your feet," he ordered.

"I just lost my son, why are you doing this?" Mary cried out.

"On your feet!" Rob repeated himself, and she slowly complied with his demand, never taking her eyes away from his.

"Phatts! Come on out, you selfish muthafucka!" Rob yelled.

"You have five seconds to bargain your life for hers!"

Phatts hated himself for underestimating the young goon. Not only did he turn the tables but he somehow was able to force information out of his most loyal and trusted friend. Seeing Skooby's body lying face down on the floor in a puddle of blood was enough to bring tears to his eyes, but nothing would hurt him more than to have anything happen to his wife and soulmate.

144

"Damn!" he cursed himself. The thought of having her caught up in his shit angered him to the core, yet made him feel nauseous all at once.

"Stop this," Mary pleaded, hoping to get through to their attacker.

"Be quiet and don't move an inch or it's over for you too." Rob warned her sternly.

"Please stop, don't you recognize me? I know you do. I saw it in your eyes just as you saw it in mine. Please stop this madness." Mary tearfully pleaded one last time.

Boom!

Rob didn't feel a lick of remorse from squeezing his trigger as he'd planned to do. Muthafuckas tried to kill him, and now the tables were turned and he was one up and ready to go all out.

"Last chance to shut up and remain still," Rob finalized his warning to the surprisingly familiar woman in his grasp.

"Muthafucka!" Phatts yelled, racing to the balcony that overlooked the foyer.

"Stop!" Mary screamed with all of her strength.

Phatts couldn't believe he'd fell for Rob's trap as he stood there fully exposed with his automatic rifle in hand. Hearing the blast from Rob's cannon made him miss his wife already, but here he stood, M16 in hand, looking down on her being used as a shield for their perpetrator.

"Phatts, get down and don't move, baby, I love you," Mary stated in her normal motherly tone.

She knew her words to her husband could've been her last but she was good with him being safe and her being in the line of fire. Slowly, she began to turn and face their attacker, but a slug from his weapon burned straight through her insides and knocked her off her feet.

The shit played in slow motion in Rob's mind. He hadn't meant to squeeze off on her but her strong sudden movement caused him to react out of reflex.

"Marrry!" Phatts yelled, rising from his low position up stairs and released a hell storm of fire from his weapon, destroying everything in his path.

Rob barely escaped the foyer with his life, diving behind a wall for cover. Phatts remained relentless in his attack, only letting up as he made it to his downed wife and friend. Blood pooled around her body as he dropped to his knees and held her tight in his arms. He rocked her hard in an attempt to wake her while calling out to her.

"Owwww!" Mary moaned in agony as he held her.

"Baby, stay with me, I'm here—I got you," Phatts cried softly.

"You—two have to stop this," she persisted.

"Why are you talking like that?" Phatts cared nothing for the people responsible for killing his son. There was no mercy nor forgiveness inside of him and he intended to make them all pay for murdering his seed.

"He—he's my—arghh," Mary struggled with her words. The pain of the gunshot wound was excruciating, nothing like she'd ever felt before.

"Stop talking, love, I gotta get you outta here and to a hospital," Phatts stated but knew there was only one problem with that statement and he'd taken his focus off of him.

"Don't think I'ma be able to allow that," Rob said as he pressed the business end of his weapon against the base of Phatts' skull.

"Listen, young blood, you can kill me now or kill me later, just please save my wife, she don't deserve to go out like this," Phatts pleaded and meant every word. He was tired of going to war with mu'fuckas and getting the people he loved taken out over his actions and mistakes. Looking over at Skooby's stretched out body was confirmation enough for him that something had to change even if it meant he'd to sacrifice himself to make it happen.

146

"No-nobody's dying—Ro-Robert Antonio-Williams, you stop with all this madness." The broken sound of his full government name being used shocked him to no words.

Thinking back all throughout his life, people always addressed him by his uncle's last name and never tried to mention his middle name because he never gave it out to anyone. To the world he was a Demps, Elijah's Demps' nephew. Elijah wasn't his blood relative but was as close as one could get through marriage. Rob always wondered how he was being raised by his uncle and not his parents. After years of lies and half-truths, he decided that he had no parents and he was his only family. He gave his uncle as much respect as one could under the circumstances but Rob could never look at him as he would a father, his father. In the mind of a young child he felt like no one really loved him if his own parents didn't love him enough to be there for him and love him like he loved them without ever even knowing them. So to him his family was dead and he was all that he had.

Now, here he stood with the deadliest intentions hearing a name that no one on earth could have known had it not been the person who gave it to him. That name was a ghost to even his uncle—Elijah. This woman really had his attention now.

"How do you know that name?" Rob asked with his weapon once again trained on her. He needed answers and he needed them quick.

"I love you, son—I've always loved you!" Mary cried out before things went black.

"Mary, baby—no, baby, wake up! I need you, ma, wake up for me. What do you mean—baby, please get up!" Phatts cried hard as his attempts to once again shake her back to consciousness failed.

Rob could not believe his ears had just heard what his mind was trying desperately to process. Son? She called him her son. How could that be after all these years of yearning to have his family.

"You—muthafucka! You killed her!" Phatts yelled in a blind fury while clicking away at his spent weapon.

Rob's eyes flinched from the sounds of Phatts finger firing away at the trigger of his assault rifle. His body was frozen in time, emotions roaring inside of him that he'd never before experienced. He didn't know what to do or how to react to anything.

"Son? You ain't no son of hers!" Phatts shouted, striking him in the head with his weapon.

"Fuck!" Rob grunted from the power of the blow before he hit the floor. His mind was on another note as Phatts had his way with him.

What did she mean by calling me her son? This can't be real. I'll wake up any second. I can't believe I shot my own mom, no fuckin' way, she ain't my mom. But how did she know my name when no one else does?

These thoughts ran rapidly through Rob's mind as he did his best to shield himself from the merciless attack Phatts was delivering. Fatigue caused Phatts to drop his weapon but the pride inside of him wouldn't pull back on the overs and unders he tried connecting with every part of Rob's face and body.

"Ba-babe," Phatts paused after hearing the gargled sound of Mary calling out to him.

"Baby, I thought I lost you," Phatts rushed to her side, outta breath.

"Should I call an ambulance?" Rob asked, not thinking clearly but really trying to help.

"Go ahead so they can do mouth to mouth with my best friend over there," Phatts replied, agitated by the sound of Rob's voice.

"Grab some keys, any of them," Phatts ordered as he gathered a second wind while carefully picking his wife up from the floor. She groaned from the sharp pains she was feeling but squeezed her eye shut in order to manage. Rob rushed to the shelf on the wall that held six sets of keys and grabbed the ones with the Bentley symbol on it. He rushed behind Phatts into the huge showroom-like garage, then quickly pressed the automatic start to fire up the vehicle. Phatts carefully laid Mary out in the back seat, then ordered Rob to sit with her before threatening to take his life if his wife lost hers. Seconds later, Phatts was on the road driving like they were racing in the Daytona 500.

"I missed you so much," Mary whispered through the pain as she looked up into Rob's eyes as he held her.

"Try notta talk, you'll need all your energy," Rob replied simply because he didn't know what else to say. There was a lot that needed to be explained but now was definitely not the time.

"I forgive you, son, I know you didn't mean to shoot me," her words caused his eyes to mist over, and he fought hard to hold them in, but the dam broke and tears streamed his cheeks as he stared down into her wet red eyes.

"Everything will be okay, just hold on for me, we got a lot to talk about." Rob couldn't believe he was feeling this way towards a complete stranger. Something inside of him told him he should believe her, but he was having a hard time accepting it. Until he could find clarity, he wasn't sure how things would be.

Chapter Thirteen

Transitioning from city jail back into the real world was such a relief for Young Mack. He hated being locked up, and understood that his situation was only beginning, but he'd rather fight it as a free man than to take his chances fighting it from behind bars. After seeing the judge, his bail was set at two hundred and fifty thousand dollars, and with Aeriella on standby—thanks to his mom—he was out and on bond within no time. He welcomed it all in. Boy, was he happy to be back home!

"Let me get this straight—They found my gun on the scene and not to mention my car and you still think you can beat this thing," Young Mack shook his head amazed at how confident Aeriella was in her abilities to get the court to see things from a different perspective. He was studying her in every way as she went over her notes, and to say that he wasn't impressed with the woman she'd become would be a flat out lie. He was really digging her in so many ways but chose not to speak on it.

They were sitting inside of *Houston's*, enjoying each other's presence while going over his case.

"Your weapon was there, true, but it was never fired. On top of that, it's not the murder weapon in this case. The car would be a whole different issue and the easiest to shy away from. We'll simply explain to the courts about your mother's sickness and have her testify, if need be, on releasing the vehicle to a group of street corner hustlers for drugs. The car being in her name would only set our case in stone." Aeriella ran it down to him in her usual confident demeanor. He loved that about her.

"Nawl, we can't go dragging my mom into this," Young Mack replied. He released a long sigh while hoping that there was another way to make their case as solid as the idea of bringing his mom in on it.

"You can't possibly drag me into my own idea, son," Young Mack looked up and met eyes with his mother after hearing her voice.

Seeing her there instantly brought a million emotions rushing in on him at one time. It had been some time since he last rode by her normal spot to hang out and get high with her friends, and to see her now only inches away from him sent chills up his arms and chest. He loved his parents with every inch of his heart, and nothing in life would ever change that.

"Ma wh-what are you doing here?" He stumbled over his words. Her frame was at an all-time low, and it showed everywhere. A lone tear escaped his eye as he took in her bony cheekbones while reaching out for her frail hand.

"Had to bring my daughter-in-law back her vehicle," Sylvia replied. She wiped his tear away with her thumb and dried the stream it left on his cheek.

"Come on, ma, why you always gotta put us together? You know we're not kids anymore!" Young Mack playfully whined as he squeezed her small frame.

"Boy, hush! I ain't putting y'all together," Sylvia smiled as she took a seat at their table and winked at Aeriella.

Young Mack shook his head while smiling at his mother. In spite of her addiction and major weight loss, his mother was still beautiful to him in every way. What her body lacked, her beauty made up for.

"Allah put y'all together, not me," Aeriella couldn't restrain her laughter after hearing Ms. Sylvia poking at Young Mack. She was enjoying his embarrassment, plus he looked so handsome to her when his face portrayed his shyness.

"Oh it's funny to you, huh?" Young Mack chuckled with them.

"I mean come on, son you two are meant to be to-gether. Besides, she's newly single and she thinks you're so cute and sexy, right, Aeriella?" It was Young Mack's turn to laugh, and boy, did he get his rocks off!

Aeriella blushed so hard that she began to sweat a little. Ms. Sylvia had put her on the spot with her own words, and there was no way for her to hide from them.

"Ms. Sylvia!" Aeriella swatted her on the hand.

"Whaaat? I'm just telling the truth. Those were your words, not mine." Young Mack bellowed in laughter, caus-ing people around the establishment to laugh with him.

"Stop laughing at me, Mackentosh!" Aeriella whined and threw a piece of breadstick his way.

"I'm sorry, love, I didn't know you felt that way about the king." He laughed some more.

"Prince," his mother corrected him.

"Haaa haa, small fry!" Aeriella joked.

"Compared to my father, everyone is a small fry in my eyes, so I'll take that title gracefully," Young Mack said, agreeing with his mother.

He knew how much his mother cared about his father and how tightly he held on to their time as king and queen of Houston's underworld.

"How is he?" Sylvia asked as a tear cascaded down her cheek. She spent most of her days concerned about her king, but could never will herself to go to that place to see him, not in her condition.

"He's huge. He works out all the time trying to stay healthy and sane. He's good, ma, no worries there!" Young Mack confirmed.

"Glad to know at least one of us is," Sylvia stated, and more tears flooded her face as her dam erupted.

"It's cool, ma, you'll come around when you're ready," Young Mack reached over and held her hand.

"I'm tired, Baby Mack, I'm tired." Sylvia sighed as tears continued to escape her eyes.

Young Mack had waited for years to hear her say those words. Nothing in life could have made him feel better than the moment he heard those words leave her lips.

"What you saying, ma?" He asked to be sure she meant what he thought she did.

"Moma is so tired. I wanna be me again. I wanna be the queen that your father built me up to be, but I'm just so weak without him, I need him sooo bad. My bones hurt more and more the longer he's away from me. I need him to just hold me and make me feel like the world revolves around me like he always did." Sylvia cried as Young Mack moved over and took her in his arms.

Aeriella's tears flowed like water from a faucet as she witnessed Sylvia's breakdown. She admired her all of her childhood. It hurt her deeply to see her so weak, fragile and vulnerable.

"It's okay, ma, I'm here—I got you, let's go home." Young Mack did his best to comfort her.

"No! I can't go there, Baby Mack, that place haunts me every time I see it." Sylvia pulled away and refused to be in the home his father left for them. Young Mack hadn't been to that house in years; he actually forgot about it until that very moment.

"Not there, ma, I wanna take you to my place until we can get you situated in any facility you can think of. I'm talking top-of-the-line facilities anywhere around the world. I'll give anything to have you back at your best." His mother fell into his embrace after hearing those words. He held her tight while escorting her to the rental Aeriella had for him.

"Follow me," he turned to face Aeriella who was taking care of their bill. She nodded her agreement before following them out of there.

"I got you, ma," Young Mack promised as he buckled her into the passenger seat. Her eyes shut, and sleep found her the moment her body touched the cushioned leather.

***

"Robert!" Mary yelled, waking from a bad dream.

"I'm here," Rob answered from his seat in the corner of her hospital room. He'd been there all night and day patiently waiting for her to wake from her sleep.

"We're here, Love." Phatts rubbed her hand from his seat next to her bed.

The tension filled her room and could be cut with a knife, and she felt it the moment she heard her husband's voice. She knew she had a lot to explain to both men sitting there together in the same room after her successful surgery.

"How long have I been out?" she asked, feeling groggy from the pain medicine flowing through her IV.

"A couple of days—you've been in and out of it and we've been here the whole time," Phatts explained.

"Oh God! I know you two have so many questions and I pray that my answers will suffice your curiosity." Mary spoke softly.

"Damn right I got some questions," Rob quickly jumped up from his seat.

"Watch yo damn mouth muth—" Phatts stood but his wife's hand calmed his approach enough for him to take his seat. "Don't ever disrespect my wife, you got me!"

"It's okay, baby, I know he's in so much pain and I'm open to answer whatever it is you need to know." Mary sympathized with Rob's rudeness because she knew he was hurting just as she had when she realized she had lost him to her family and then to the system.

"I paid a nurse to give us a DNA test while you were out of it, here." Rob tossed the papers on her legs.

She didn't even make a move for them because she knew deep down that he was her son. Phatts, however, couldn't wait to get his hands on those papers. He wasn't sure where his wife had consumed a child from, or with whom she'd shared herself with, but he was hoping that Rob wasn't her son so that he could finish what he started and achieve what Skooby had failed to.

"Shit!" Phatts exhaled, tossing the results on the hospital room floor.

"First thing I wanna know is who my father is," Rob's eyes misted over as he stared down on his injured mother. The mother that he himself had put a bullet through.

The look in Mary's eyes said it all as tears rolled down her face on both sides. She looked to the man she'd loved for as long as she could possibly remember. He was the first man she'd ever given herself to, but Mary was a good girl, and after finding out about his lifestyle in the streets back then, she just couldn't stay with him knowing he'd end up hurting her. She knew in the life there was only jail or death lying in wait, and she wanted no parts of either at her young age.

Months had passed after giving herself to him before she found out she was pregnant with his baby, but how could she go back to him knowing she would be putting not only herself but their child in danger by being close to him. As selfish as it was, she chose to keep her baby her little secret; that was until her money-hungry, drug addict mother figured it out and took full advantage of her situation.

"You kept this away from me all these years?" Phatts erupted in anger and complete disbelief.

"I had no choice," Mary replied, barely above a whisper.

"Yeah, you had one and you made it for the both of us," Phatts grabbed his keys and stormed out of the room, not before stopping to get a good look at Rob. He shook his head at how similar his boys were to one another. His heart ached from the loss of his young son, and he wasn't finished making the streets pay for taking him away, and to find out now that he had a son from his heydays was something he didn't know how to feel about.

"She took you away from me," Mary cried.

Rob wasn't sure what to do. The sight and sound of her cries was making him feel some type of way. She was his mother, the mother he cried so many nights to have hold him and care for him and tell him that everything was gonna be alright. She was there now after all these years of yearning, and he wasn't sure what to do to console her. She had been through some tough times in life just as he had, and now they were together, and he wanted desperately to make something of it.

'She tricked me into going to college and promised she'd take good care of you. She was the one who put you in foster care system and told those people I had abandoned you and she didn't know where I was. That was after no one wanted to pay her for child to support her drug habits." Mary continued to cry.

"How could someone do that to their child and grand-child?" Rob felt sick listening to a past that had tortured his mother and resulted to his growing up with a man he barely knew.

"God, you gotta forgive me, I never thought I'd see you again. I actually smiled the day she was taken away from this earth. She had hurt me beyond repair. For so many years she treated me like dirt, like I was less than a human, like I wasn't her own flesh and blood." Mary cringed thinking back on a time so long ago.

"I blamed you for so many years and now to hear this, I just don't know how to feel." Rob sighed as he took a seat next to her hospital bed, rubbing his face with both hands.

"Blame me, I can take that as long as I know that you forgive me for being so weak and losing you. I need you to forgive me for not being able to find you for so long. I saw pictures but no known addresses or contact numbers, but I knew it was you from the moment I saw you walk through that door." Rob sat there not knowing how to forgive a woman he didn't even know until he nearly killed her days ago.

"I forgive you, but are you sure he's my father?" Rob chuckled while taking her hand in his.

"Ninety-nine point nine percent, he's the only man I've ever given myself to in my entire life," Mary confessed.

Facts were facts, and Phatts was indeed his father, no matter how much he hated it or how badly he wanted to kill Phatts for ordering his death. This changed everything.

***

"A fuckin' son I never knew about," Phatts slammed his shot glass against the bar in his home.

He took his time trying to drink himself into a coma to forget about all the things that were happening. After cleaning things up alongside two of his trusted men (the spot where Skooby had taken his last breath), he'd been stuck there at his wet bar ever since. Reality was kicking him in the ass, and there was nothing he could do to stop it.

"I said you guys could leave once everything was done!" he stated after hearing slow footsteps enter the room. He remained slouched at the bar with his back to the door, listening to the deep breathing in the silence of the room.

"I guess you came to finish the job, huh?" Phatts knew immediately after not getting a response who was there, or so he thought.

"We had an agreement," the deep familiar voice stated and sent chills rushing all over Phatts' body. His eyes nearly popped outta his head when he turned and locked eyes with the bogey man himself.

"G-Gator-I-Man, listen, I tried reaching you—" Phatts staggered as urine threatened to pop his bladder.

"I-I-don't want no trouble, I'll even double our normal agreement right here right now," Phatts pleaded as Gator advanced towards him.

"This ain't about no damn money, you damn money junkie!" Gator growled while wrapping his left hand around Phatts' throat, nearly crushing his windpipe.

"You touched Young Mack, more than once, knowing there would be consequences. Well, I'm consequence." Gator squeezed tighter, cutting Phatts' air supply in half.

"You touched my family, but I'll spare your wife for the blood of your son is on the hands of my family. Her life will not be harmed," Gator promised while squeezing harder as Phatts tried desperately to escape his grip. Gator added pressure to his death grip and crushed the bones in Phatts' neck, causing his head to slope grotesquely to the side before Gator let his body hit the floor.

***

Rob couldn't believe the news as it was being delivered. Mary clung to him, devastated by the news of her husband's murder along with two of his men at their home. Neither of them could understand why the officers were there questioning them as if they committed the murders themselves. Their shitty attitudes quickly became too much for Rob's taste, and he politely asked the rude officers to exit the room.

He did his best to console his mother because it pained him something serious to see her hurting. He couldn't share her feelings for Phatts' death but he felt all of her pain. Phatts was his pops, but he never got to know him as such. Hell, they were enemies because Phatts had ordered his death for some reason that he had yet to find out why.

"I don't know what I'm gonna do without him," Mary spoke, snapping him from his thoughts.

"W-uh—it's gonna be alright, ma," Rob said, not knowing how things were gonna turn out for them.

"I need to know what happened to them, Robert, I need to know what happened at that house."

"The officers told us what happened when they were here," he reminded her.

"No! I need to know everything. I know you don't know him as your father, but he is my husband and I need to know what happened and why he isn't here with us." She began to cry all over again.

"How are we gonna find out what really took place?" Rob asked, confused.

"We have one helluva surveillance system hidden all around that house—he made sure of it!" Mary confirmed.

Rob sat there thinking to himself for a few minutes before agreeing to visit their home to go over the murder footage.

"Please be honest with your findings, I'm a big girl. I can take it however it comes." Mary forced a smile before wrapping her arms around his neck.

"I got you." He agreed before leaving her hospital room.

He had to admit to himself that shit was crazy as fuck all around him. Since the day his team took their first loss, nothing had been the same. He thought back to the robbery he pulled off with Ash and Max, and remembered Max's face when he showed up to end his life for running off with their winnings. He even thought back to the moment he was issued a death sentence by the man he just found out was his biological father after he forced himself inside of his home to kill him. He thought about how he had shot a woman, the wife of the man he'd come to kill, who turned out to be his mother.

Now he was pulling up to their home for the second time, this time to investigate the murder of his father by hands other than his. Looking out at the beautiful brick home, one would never guess that so much drama had occurred there in the past week.

Rob took a breath as he stepped inside of the house. He exhaled slowly while making his way through the kitchen from the garage entrance. The gloomy home was cold but all intact as nothing seemed out of order besides the many holes in the walls caused by the shootout he'd had with his father. He thought back to his close escape while having visions of the moment he pulled the trigger that sent a hot slug through his mother's stomach.

Shaking those visions from his mind, he made his way up the stairs and into the master bedroom. He looked around the spacious room which held a small kitchen with all the appliances necessary for a full-sized kitchen. A Jacuzzi was on the floor, and a huge flat screen nearly took up the far wall of the room. Before him was a California-king sized bed angled on top of what looked to be a real tiger's fur and stuffed head.

He moved next to the bed and opened the drawer that Mary told him would hold a key to the secret room where he would find the home's security surveillance monitors. He reached in and took the key out before stepping into the bedroom's walk-in closet where he moved things around and found the door to the secret room exactly where she said it would be.

Once inside, he saw the station with the high-tech computer screen monitors all connected in one way or another. Each screen played four different angles at once, there was even a monitor showing himself standing where he currently was. He took a seat and observed the keyboard. It held a handwritten footnote for every button's operation. He searched until he found the key that read MAIN MENU, then held it down like the footnote instructed. He flinched as all the monitors slid in place and created one big screen showing the main menu and all of its options.

"High-tech shit," Rob said out loud and smiled.

"High tech shit is not an option, please state a visible optional request." The automated voice coming from the computer blew him away.

This the type of shit a broke mufucka would never bear witness to, he thought to himself.

He read over each option carefully and selected the one he needed in order to go over the footage of his father's murder. The system asked for a password, and once given, it quickly showed his chosen option. Frozen images of the previously recorded footage came on the screen and he immediately held down the button to rewind it. Images flashed by the screen at a super-fast rate, but he stopped it long before the officers said Phatts arrived back at the house. He pressed *play,* and the sixteen monitors paired in fours and separated from a single image, and showed views from all angles. There were even angles from up the block. He fast-forwarded it until that moment Phatts was pulling up into the house.

Shortly after Phatts arrived, a black tinted out Chevy Tahoe pulled into the driveway and two men exited the vehicle.

"Clean-up crew," Rob said to himself as he watched the footage.

He watched as Phatts and his men grotesquely chopped up and disposed of Skooby's body. It amazed him that Phatts involved himself in a job clearly meant for his workers, especially a job that would destroy any evidence that Rob killed his man. Doing away with Skooby's body would keep anything from coming back on his killer, and Rob watched as Phatts ran the show and protected his flesh and blood.

He watched as Phatts' workers carefully carried a barrel marked with the hazardous chemical symbol. With rubber gloves and respirators on their face, limb by bloody limb, the men placed the mutilated body parts inside of the barrel of what he guessed to be some sort of chemical acid. The process of getting rid of Skooby's body didn't take long, and the men were soon walking the barrel back out into the garage where they lifted it and put it into the back of the Chevy, which he noted was still in the garage.

Suddenly, he thought he saw movement in the monitors above the garage footage, but nothing was there. After a few seconds, he went back to watching the garage footage, and there was blood everywhere. Rob was so caught up in the moment he leaped from his seat in shock. Both men in the garage held their oozing throats while simultaneously trying desperately to hold in their intestines from the gaping holes in their stomachs. The scene was a gruesome one, and he had to tear his eyes away. Phatts was sitting at the bar with his back to the hidden surveillance camera, only a few feet away from his dying men out in the garage.

Everything was still besides the times on the cameras. He watched as Phatts turned around in a panic-stricken shock, moments before a huge figure approached him. Phatts seemed to be mouthing something before the giant guy took him by the throat. Rob hurried to find the right button to get the audio working. Going back to main menu, the screens rushed together as if they understood his haste. He found the sound option and set it at maximum level before rewinding the footage once again.

This time he listened closely as Phatts pleaded with the man he'd called 'Gator'. Rob recognized the name immediately. It was a mythical one, and now he realized that the fear of the myth was actual fear of a true being. He was in awe.

Rob watched as Gator grabbed Phatts by the throat with speed like nothing he'd ever seen before. He flinched when Gator's face came into view behind the bar. The sight of him was shocking to say the least; he really resembled the amphibious reptile he got his name from. As shocking as the true physical being of a myth come to reality was, nothing could have prepared Rob for the words that came outta Gator's mouth.

"Young Mack?" Rob said out loud and sat up in his seat confused.

He tried hard to figure out where Young Mack came into play and what role he played in the murder of his father. Phatts had issued him a death sentence because of something Young Mack was involved in, and now here it was that Phatts was issued his death sentence and put to rest in the name of Young Mack. Shit just did not add up. Before today, nothing really mattered to Rob, but today had happened and the playing field had changed. Phatts was his father; it was still his flesh and blood and Young Mack was the reason he'd never get to know his father in ways that he always dreamed of.

"You gotta answer for this shit, Young Mack!" Rob fumed as he sat back and replayed the entire video.

To be Continued—

Coming Soon—
P.O.T.S. 2

Lock Down Publications and Ca$h Presents
Assisted Publishing Packages

BASIC PACKAGE	UPGRADED PACKAGE
$499	$800
Editing	Typing
Cover Design	Editing
Formatting	Cover Design
	Formatting
ADVANCE PACKAGE	**LDP SUPREME PACKAGE**
$1,200	$1,500
Typing	Typing
Editing	Editing
Cover Design	Cover Design
Formatting	Formatting
Copyright registration	Copyright registration
Proofreading	Proofreading
Upload book to Amazon	Set up Amazon account
	Upload book to Amazon
	Advertise on LDP, Amazon and Facebook Page

***Other services available upon request.
Additional charges may apply
Lock Down Publications
P.O. Box 944
Stockbridge, GA 30281-9998
Phone: 470 303-9761

Submission Guideline

Submit the first three chapters of your completed manuscript to ldpsubmissions@gmail.com, subject line: Your book's title. The manuscript must be in a .doc file and sent as an attachment. Document should be in Times New Roman, double spaced and in size 12 font. Also, provide your synopsis and full contact information. If sending multiple submissions, they must each be in a separate email.

Have a story but no way to send it electronically? You can still submit to LDP/Ca$h Presents. Send in the first three chapters, written or typed, of your completed manuscript to:

LDP: Submissions Dept
Po Box 944
Stockbridge, Ga 30281

DO NOT send original manuscript. Must be a duplicate.

Provide your synopsis and a cover letter containing your full contact information.

Thanks for considering LDP and Ca$h Presents.

NEW RELEASES

SOSA GANG 2 by ROMELL TUKES
KINGZ OF THE GAME 7 by PLAYA RAY
SKI MASK MONEY 2 by RENTA
BORN IN THE GRAVE 3 by SELF MADE TAY
LOYALTY IS EVERYTHING 3 by MOLOTTI

Coming Soon from Lock Down Publications/Ca$h Presents

BLOOD OF A BOSS **VI**
SHADOWS OF THE GAME II
TRAP BASTARD II
By Askari
LOYAL TO THE GAME **IV**
By T.J. & Jelissa
TRUE SAVAGE **VIII**
MIDNIGHT CARTEL IV
DOPE BOY MAGIC IV
CITY OF KINGZ III
NIGHTMARE ON SILENT AVE II
THE PLUG OF LIL MEXICO II
CLASSIC CITY II
By Chris Green
BLAST FOR ME **III**
A SAVAGE DOPEBOY III
CUTTHROAT MAFIA III
DUFFLE BAG CARTEL VII
HEARTLESS GOON VI
By Ghost
A HUSTLER'S DECEIT III
KILL ZONE II
BAE BELONGS TO ME III
TIL DEATH II
By Aryanna
KING OF THE TRAP III
By T.J. Edwards
GORILLAZ IN THE BAY V
3X KRAZY III
STRAIGHT BEAST MODE III

De'Kari
KINGPIN KILLAZ IV
STREET KINGS III
PAID IN BLOOD III
CARTEL KILLAZ IV
DOPE GODS III
Hood Rich
SINS OF A HUSTLA II
ASAD
YAYO V
Bred In The Game 2
S. Allen
THE STREETS WILL TALK II
By Yolanda Moore
SON OF A DOPE FIEND III
HEAVEN GOT A GHETTO III
SKI MASK MONEY III
By Renta
LOYALTY AIN'T PROMISED III
By Keith Williams
I'M NOTHING WITHOUT HIS LOVE II
SINS OF A THUG II
TO THE THUG I LOVED BEFORE II
IN A HUSTLER I TRUST II
By Monet Dragun
QUIET MONEY IV
EXTENDED CLIP III
THUG LIFE IV
By Trai'Quan
THE STREETS MADE ME IV
By Larry D. Wright
IF YOU CROSS ME ONCE III
ANGEL V
By Anthony Fields

THE STREETS WILL NEVER CLOSE IV
By K'ajji
HARD AND RUTHLESS III
KILLA KOUNTY IV
By Khufu
MONEY GAME III
By Smoove Dolla
JACK BOYS VS DOPE BOYS IV
A GANGSTA'S QUR'AN V
COKE GIRLZ II
COKE BOYS II
LIFE OF A SAVAGE V
CHI'RAQ GANGSTAS V
SOSA GANG III
BRONX SAVAGES II
BODYMORE KINGPINS II
By Romell Tukes
MURDA WAS THE CASE III
Elijah R. Freeman
AN UNFORESEEN LOVE IV
BABY, I'M WINTERTIME COLD III
By Meesha

QUEEN OF THE ZOO III
By Black Migo
CONFESSIONS OF A JACKBOY III
By Nicholas Lock
KING KILLA II
By Vincent "Vitto" Holloway
BETRAYAL OF A THUG III
By Fre$h
THE MURDER QUEENS III
By Michael Gallon
THE BIRTH OF A GANGSTER III
By Delmont Player
TREAL LOVE II

By Le'Monica Jackson
FOR THE LOVE OF BLOOD III
By Jamel Mitchell
RAN OFF ON DA PLUG II
By Paper Boi Rari
HOOD CONSIGLIERE III
By Keese
PRETTY GIRLS DO NASTY THINGS II
By Nicole Goosby
PROTÉGÉ OF A LEGEND III
LOVE IN THE TRENCHES II
By Corey Robinson
IT'S JUST ME AND YOU II
By Ah'Million
FOREVER GANGSTA III
By Adrian Dulan
GORILLAZ IN THE TRENCHES II
By SayNoMore
THE COCAINE PRINCESS VIII
By King Rio
CRIME BOSS II
Playa Ray
LOYALTY IS EVERYTHING III
Molotti
HERE TODAY GONE TOMORROW II
By Fly Rock
REAL G'S MOVE IN SILENCE II
By Von Diesel
GRIMEY WAYS IV
By Ray Vinci

Available Now

RESTRAINING ORDER **I & II**
By CA$H & Coffee
LOVE KNOWS NO BOUNDARIES **I II & III**
By Coffee
RAISED AS A GOON I, II, III & IV
BRED BY THE SLUMS I, II, III
BLAST FOR ME I & II
ROTTEN TO THE CORE I II III
A BRONX TALE I, II, III
DUFFLE BAG CARTEL I II III IV V VI
HEARTLESS GOON I II III IV V
A SAVAGE DOPEBOY I II
DRUG LORDS I II III
CUTTHROAT MAFIA I II
KING OF THE TRENCHES
By Ghost
LAY IT DOWN **I & II**
LAST OF A DYING BREED I II
BLOOD STAINS OF A SHOTTA I & II III
By Jamaica
LOYAL TO THE GAME I II III
LIFE OF SIN I, II III
By TJ & Jelissa
BLOODY COMMAS I & II
SKI MASK CARTEL I II & III
KING OF NEW YORK I II,III IV V
RISE TO POWER I II III
COKE KINGS I II III IV V
BORN HEARTLESS I II III IV
KING OF THE TRAP I II
By T.J. Edwards

IF LOVING HIM IS WRONG…I & II
LOVE ME EVEN WHEN IT HURTS I II III
By Jelissa
WHEN THE STREETS CLAP BACK I & II III
THE HEART OF A SAVAGE I II III IV
MONEY MAFIA I II
LOYAL TO THE SOIL I II III
By Jibril Williams
A DISTINGUISHED THUG STOLE MY HEART I II
& III
LOVE SHOULDN'T HURT I II III IV
RENEGADE BOYS I II III IV
PAID IN KARMA I II III
SAVAGE STORMS I II III
AN UNFORESEEN LOVE I II III
BABY, I'M WINTERTIME COLD I II
By Meesha
A GANGSTER'S CODE I &, II III
A GANGSTER'S SYN I II III
THE SAVAGE LIFE I II III
CHAINED TO THE STREETS I II III
BLOOD ON THE MONEY I II III
A GANGSTA'S PAIN I II III
By J-Blunt
PUSH IT TO THE LIMIT
By Bre' Hayes
BLOOD OF A BOSS I, II, III, IV, V
SHADOWS OF THE GAME
TRAP BASTARD
By Askari
THE STREETS BLEED MURDER **I, II & III**
THE HEART OF A GANGSTA I II& III
By Jerry Jackson
CUM FOR ME I II III IV V VI VII VIII

An LDP Erotica Collaboration
BRIDE OF A HUSTLA **I II & II**
THE FETTI GIRLS **I, II& III**
CORRUPTED BY A GANGSTA I, II III, IV
BLINDED BY HIS LOVE
THE PRICE YOU PAY FOR LOVE I, II ,III
DOPE GIRL MAGIC I II III
By Destiny Skai
WHEN A GOOD GIRL GOES BAD
By Adrienne
THE COST OF LOYALTY I II III
By Kweli
A GANGSTER'S REVENGE **I II III & IV**
THE BOSS MAN'S DAUGHTERS I II III IV V
A SAVAGE LOVE **I & II**
BAE BELONGS TO ME I II
A HUSTLER'S DECEIT I, II, III
WHAT BAD BITCHES DO I, II, III
SOUL OF A MONSTER I II III
KILL ZONE
A DOPE BOY'S QUEEN I II III
TIL DEATH
By Aryanna
A KINGPIN'S AMBITON
A KINGPIN'S AMBITION **II**
I MURDER FOR THE DOUGH
By Ambitious
TRUE SAVAGE I II III IV V VI VII
DOPE BOY MAGIC I, II, III
MIDNIGHT CARTEL I II III
CITY OF KINGZ I II
NIGHTMARE ON SILENT AVE
THE PLUG OF LIL MEXICO II
CLASSIC CITY
By Chris Green
A DOPEBOY'S PRAYER

By Eddie "Wolf" Lee
THE KING CARTEL **I, II & III**
By Frank Gresham
THESE NIGGAS AIN'T LOYAL **I, II & III**
By Nikki Tee
GANGSTA SHYT **I II &III**
By CATO
THE ULTIMATE BETRAYAL
By Phoenix
Boss'n Up i , ii & IIi
By Royal Nicole
I LOVE YOU TO DEATH
By Destiny J
I RIDE FOR MY HITTA
I STILL RIDE FOR MY HITTA
By Misty Holt
LOVE & CHASIN' PAPER
By Qay Crockett
TO DIE IN VAIN
SINS OF A HUSTLA
By ASAD
BROOKLYN HUSTLAZ
By Boogsy Morina
BROOKLYN ON LOCK I & II
By Sonovia
GANGSTA CITY
By Teddy Duke
A DRUG KING AND HIS DIAMOND I & II III
A DOPEMAN'S RICHES
HER MAN, MINE'S TOO I, II
CASH MONEY HO'S
THE WIFEY I USED TO BE I II
PRETTY GIRLS DO NASTY THINGS
By Nicole Goosby

TRAPHOUSE KING **I II & III**
KINGPIN KILLAZ I II III
STREET KINGS I II
PAID IN BLOOD **I II**
CARTEL KILLAZ I II III
DOPE GODS I II
By Hood Rich
LIPSTICK KILLAH **I, II, III**
CRIME OF PASSION I II & III
FRIEND OR FOE I II III
By Mimi
STEADY MOBBN' **I, II, III**
THE STREETS STAINED MY SOUL I II III
By Marcellus Allen
WHO SHOT YA **I, II, III**
SON OF A DOPE FIEND I II
HEAVEN GOT A GHETTO I II
SKI MASK MONEY I II
Renta
GORILLAZ IN THE BAY **I II III IV**
TEARS OF A GANGSTA I II
3X KRAZY I II
STRAIGHT BEAST MODE I II
DE'KARI
TRIGGADALE I II III
MURDAROBER WAS THE CASE I II
Elijah R. Freeman
GOD BLESS THE TRAPPERS I, II, III
THESE SCANDALOUS STREETS I, II, III
FEAR MY GANGSTA I, II, III IV, V
THESE STREETS DON'T LOVE NOBODY I, II
BURY ME A G I, II, III, IV, V
A GANGSTA'S EMPIRE I, II, III, IV
THE DOPEMAN'S BODYGAURD I II
THE REALEST KILLAZ I II III
THE LAST OF THE OGS I II III

Tranay Adams
THE STREETS ARE CALLING
Duquie Wilson
MARRIED TO A BOSS I II III
By Destiny Skai & Chris Green
KINGZ OF THE GAME I II III IV V VI VII
CRIME BOSS
Playa Ray
SLAUGHTER GANG I II III
RUTHLESS HEART I II III
By Willie Slaughter
FUK SHYT
By Blakk Diamond
DON'T F#CK WITH MY HEART I II
By Linnea
ADDICTED TO THE DRAMA I II III
IN THE ARM OF HIS BOSS II
By Jamila
YAYO I II III IV
A SHOOTER'S AMBITION I II
BRED IN THE GAME
By S. Allen
TRAP GOD I II III
RICH $AVAGE I II III
MONEY IN THE GRAVE I II III
By Martell Troublesome Bolden
FOREVER GANGSTA I II
 GLOCKS ON SATIN SHEETS I II
By Adrian Dulan
TOE TAGZ I II III IV
LEVELS TO THIS SHYT I II
IT'S JUST ME AND YOU
By Ah'Million
KINGPIN DREAMS I II III

RAN OFF ON DA PLUG
By Paper Boi Rari
CONFESSIONS OF A GANGSTA I II III IV
CONFESSIONS OF A JACKBOY I II
By Nicholas Lock
I'M NOTHING WITHOUT HIS LOVE
SINS OF A THUG
TO THE THUG I LOVED BEFORE
A GANGSTA SAVED XMAS
IN A HUSTLER I TRUST
By Monet Dragun
CAUGHT UP IN THE LIFE I II III
THE STREETS NEVER LET GO I II III
By Robert Baptiste
NEW TO THE GAME I II III
MONEY, MURDER & MEMORIES I II III
By Malik D. Rice
LIFE OF A SAVAGE I II III IV
A GANGSTA'S QUR'AN I II III IV
MURDA SEASON I II III
GANGLAND CARTEL I II III
CHI'RAQ GANGSTAS I II III IV
KILLERS ON ELM STREET I II III
JACK BOYZ N DA BRONX I II III
A DOPEBOY'S DREAM I II III
JACK BOYS VS DOPE BOYS I II III
COKE GIRLZ
COKE BOYS
SOSA GANG I II
BRONX SAVAGES
BODYMORE KINGPINS
By Romell Tukes
LOYALTY AIN'T PROMISED I II
By Keith Williams
QUIET MONEY I II III
THUG LIFE I II III

EXTENDED CLIP I II
A GANGSTA'S PARADISE
By Trai'Quan
THE STREETS MADE ME I II III
By Larry D. Wright
THE ULTIMATE SACRIFICE I, II, III, IV, V, VI
KHADIFI
IF YOU CROSS ME ONCE I II
ANGEL I II III IV
IN THE BLINK OF AN EYE
By Anthony Fields
THE LIFE OF A HOOD STAR
By Ca$h & Rashia Wilson
THE STREETS WILL NEVER CLOSE I II III
By K'ajji
CREAM I II III
THE STREETS WILL TALK
By Yolanda Moore
NIGHTMARES OF A HUSTLA I II III
By King Dream
CONCRETE KILLA I II III
VICIOUS LOYALTY I II III
By Kingpen
HARD AND RUTHLESS I II
MOB TOWN 251
THE BILLIONAIRE BENTLEYS I II III
REAL G'S MOVE IN SILENCE
By Von Diesel
GHOST MOB
Stilloan Robinson
MOB TIES I II III IV V VI
SOUL OF A HUSTLER, HEART OF A KILLER I II
GORILLAZ IN THE TRENCHES
By SayNoMore

BODYMORE MURDERLAND I II III
THE BIRTH OF A GANGSTER I II
By Delmont Player
FOR THE LOVE OF A BOSS
By C. D. Blue
MOBBED UP I II III IV
THE BRICK MAN I II III IV V
THE COCAINE PRINCESS I II III IV V VI VII
By King Rio
KILLA KOUNTY I II III IV
By Khufu
MONEY GAME I II
By Smoove Dolla
A GANGSTA'S KARMA I II III
By FLAME
KING OF THE TRENCHES I II III
 by GHOST & TRANAY ADAMS
QUEEN OF THE ZOO I II
By Black Migo
GRIMEY WAYS I II III
By Ray Vinci
XMAS WITH AN ATL SHOOTER
By Ca$h & Destiny Skai
KING KILLA
By Vincent "Vitto" Holloway
BETRAYAL OF A THUG I II
By Fre$h
THE MURDER QUEENS I II
By Michael Gallon
TREAL LOVE
By Le'Monica Jackson
FOR THE LOVE OF BLOOD I II
By Jamel Mitchell
HOOD CONSIGLIERE I II
By Keese
PROTÉGÉ OF A LEGEND I II

LOVE IN THE TRENCHES
By Corey Robinson
BORN IN THE GRAVE I II III
By Self Made Tay
MOAN IN MY MOUTH
By XTASY
TORN BETWEEN A GANGSTER AND A GEN-
TLEMAN
By J-BLUNT & Miss Kim
LOYALTY IS EVERYTHING I II
Molotti
HERE TODAY GONE TOMORROW
By Fly Rock
PILLOW PRINCESS
By S. Hawkins

BOOKS BY LDP'S CEO, CA$H

TRUST IN NO MAN
TRUST IN NO MAN 2
TRUST IN NO MAN 3
BONDED BY BLOOD
SHORTY GOT A THUG
THUGS CRY
THUGS CRY 2
THUGS CRY 3
TRUST NO BITCH
TRUST NO BITCH 2
TRUST NO BITCH 3
TIL MY CASKET DROPS
RESTRAINING ORDER
RESTRAINING ORDER 2
IN LOVE WITH A CONVICT
LIFE OF A HOOD STAR
XMAS WITH AN ATL SHOOTER